Karankawa County

Karankawa County

Short Stories from a Corner of Texas

Neal Morgan

Texas A&M University Press
COLLEGE STATION

Library of Congress Cataloging-in-Publication Data
Morgan, Neal, 1934–
    Karankawa County : short stories from a corner of Texas / Neal Morgan.
        p. cm.
    ISBN 0-89096-423-8 (alk. paper)
    1. Texas—Fiction.   I. Title.
PS3563.087142K37   1990
813'.54—dc20   89-48086
                                                                                  CIP

To my family

I long ago lost a hound, a bay horse and a turtle-dove, and am still on their trail. Many are the travellers I have spoken to concerning them, describing their tracks, and what calls they answered to. I have met one or two who have heard the hound, and the tramp of the horse, and even seen the dove disappear behind a cloud; and they seemed as anxious to recover them as if they had lost them themselves.

—Henry David Thoreau

Contents

Karankawa County

About Karankawa County

The children of Karankawa County, Texas, live in a constant state of confusion.

They learn at an early age that their home country—level, damp, marshy, and mosquito-ridden—exists only in *reality*, not in the perceptions of those concerned with perpetuating Texas myths. And they're smart enough to know, from watching television, that in their world perceptions are infinitely more important than reality.

Hollywood, in its portrayal of the Sabine River, that onetime border between Mexico and Louisiana which loomed important in stories of Sam Houston and Texas' war against Santa Anna, has always confused them. In those movies, a Texas officer often dispatches a rider to Louisiana—a trip that obviously requires crossing Karankawa County and the Neches River to get to the Sabine. Karankawa County children sit eating popcorn on the edge of their seats, eagerly awaiting the rider's arrival in country they will recognize.

They are invariably disappointed. The Sabine of Hollywood is always a shallow, rocky stream bordered by cactus and mesquite.

But their confusion cannot be blamed on Hollywood alone, for Karankawa County has been lost in history and its people exist in a veritable vacuum, partly of their own creation.

Karankawa County advertises itself as "the Southeasternmost County in Texas," sits astride the confluence of the Neches River and Brand's Bayou, and extends southward to where both pour muddy water and rotten bits of Deep East Texas into the Gulf of Mexico. The advertising has never done much good. Karankawa County has gone largely unheralded in story, song, movies, and tele-

3

vision; and it's had an identity crisis since its inception in the middle nineteenth century. Such obscurity is at least partially due to a very large mistake by its namers.

The Karankawa Indians for whom the county was named never lived there.

Those Indians who did live there, the Atakapans, believed that people who got themselves eaten by other people, or died from snakebite poison, could never get into heaven. The word "Atakapa" in the Choctaw tongue means cannibal.

The founding fathers of Karankawa County had never heard of the Atakapans because there was no mention of them in books in Holland, where the founders were educated before landing on the Texas coast. So the county was named for the first tribe of Gulf Coast Indians the settlers heard of: the Karankawas.

But the Karankawas were cannibals too, so either way the Dutch would have named the county for cannibalistic Indians. Which was regrettable, and perhaps prophetic . . .

In 1901 the Lucas gusher came in near Beaumont, some twenty-five miles northwest of Karankawa County, and a lot of people got rich and oil refineries sprang up all over Southeast Texas. Karankawa County became semi-affluent, middle-class, and pragmatic. People moved in from Louisiana, Mississippi, Arkansas, and other southern states, found jobs in the refineries, and lived comfortably enough. But many—perhaps most—of them moved from nearby Deep East Texas, which is practically the same as leaving Mississippi and needs some explanation.

Pine forests cover both Mississippi and Deep East Texas, which is only a topographical-geographical consideration and doesn't do the subject justice. The affinity between the two goes much deeper. There's a dark, hooded, Faulknerian similarity, and a certain narrow, suspicious way of looking at life. In the minds of Texas coastal plainsfolk, logical or not, tree lines (mainly pine trees) best define the limits of Mississippi–Deep East Texas attitudes. Their logic implies that too many generations of living in the deep shade of pine forests somehow warps and darkens one's outlook on life.

The pines of East Texas stop in north Beaumont.

And south from there, to where Karankawa County touches the

Gulf of Mexico, the only pines standing were fairly recently planted by people who love their shadowy presence.

Karankawa County, Texas, was a vast sea of grass when the Dutch first came.

And it still would be, were it not for the first "yard-beautiful" lunatic who planted Chinese tallow trees about 1950. (Suggested, no doubt, by some national magazine more concerned with yard-piddling than ecology or the natural beauty of Karankawa County prairies.) Now Karankawa County peers out from among the tallow trees, and shows plenty of evidence of pine-tree attitudes, if not pine trees.

The county exists in a vague never-never-land, rests clouded in the minds of residents and outsiders alike, and in its obscurity remains untenably stretched between the divergent cultures of South and West. And the local media have added to the confusion.

Roughly encompassed by the cities of Beaumont, Port Arthur, and Orange, with Karankawa County near its center, the area was first called Southeast Texas. Then, with the glittering success of the oil industry in the early 1960s, it became known as the Golden Triangle. But the gold became tarnished by OPEC, and the local media arbitrarily renamed it "the Triplex." The media people said they felt the area needed a change in its "image."

Area newspapers were flooded with protests about the name change, but the outraged cries fell on deaf ears; the media persisted in calling it the Triplex. They only aggravated a century-old identity crisis.

Now nobody knows what to call it. And Karankawa County children are more confused than ever.

The cowboys and all the cattle drives on television still travel over cactus- and mesquite-covered trails, through fogs of dust and swarms of plains Indians. The oil business, the roughneck and driller, the wooden derricks of yesteryear are still set in that selfsame Texas desert. (Everything else on television, of course, happens in California.) Hollywood seems quite certain that Texas extends only from the Colorado River westward to El Paso, and Karankawa County children are still waiting for that horseman to arrive in grass stirrup-deep near the Neches and Sabine. Just once, they want to watch him cross those broad, sweeping currents, instead of wading dinky, knee-deep creeks.

And even their teachers don't tell them that the first traildrives in Texas were made from just west of the Neches—Karankawa County—to New Orleans. From 1750 to 1850 hundreds of thousands of Longhorns traveled not through mesquite, cactus, and alkali dust, but through the swamps and marshes of the Texas coastal plains. That was going on before the first Longhorn cow ever poked her nose west of Fort Worth, Texas—that legendary cowtown—but it was somehow missed by popular novelists and historical writers alike. To say nothing of Karankawa County history teachers.

How can you have pride in something you can't correctly name? If Karankawans were sure of their identity, they would hardly allow the media to decide who they are. That's basic to their problem. And a requisite change in their image must suggest there was something wrong with the one they already had.

Being an amalgam of people—Southerners and Deep East Texans, mostly—whose roots and history lie somewhere else, few of them feel any sense of continuity, *of place,* in Karankawa County. With the possible exception of third- or fourth-generation coastal plains dwellers who never had the slightest doubt of their own identities, that is.

Those coastal plains long-timers are irrevocably tied to the land, hate tallow trees and the yard-piddlers who planted them, and barely tolerate the pine-tree-transplants springing up on the prairies amongst them. Even people who have grown rich from oil still regard the great refineries and chemical plants as transient, like the workers who flocked in with them. They view themselves as *Texan,* these coastal plainsfolk, and care naught what Hollywood, novelists, or history teachers write or say. They are sure one has to really *work* at being a Texan today, in the face of technology and the influx of people (even *Yankees*) and they show thinly veiled contempt for anyone not thusly occupied.

Battles rage in Karankawa County. Between rich and poor; native and immigrant; rancher and chemist; liberal and conservative; media and private citizen. They're hotly contested on the prairies and marshes, but fiercer yet in the county's two towns: Karankawa

City, the county seat in the center of the county, and Janus Point on the Gulf of Mexico.

There was a time in Texas when stories were told around campfires, embellished by listeners, then polished and repeated by those among them who were the best storytellers. This was, in its own way, the literature of the plains, and it often ended up in print after having been smoothed, rounded, and burnished to a high sheen in much the same way a stone is made lustrous by years in a rushing river. At least that's what Texas writers have said.

So what happened in Karankawa County?

Maybe the mosquitoes were too bad. Perhaps wood was too scarce, or too wet, for campfires; or the people too worn out to tell stories back then. And perchance that is the reason nobody outside Southeast Texas has ever heard of Karankawa County.

But stories are told in Karankawa County today. The following are repeated—not around campfires, of course, but at house parties of the semi-affluent. Or in redneck beer joints of the less fortunate.

Or by Coach Jacobs, who is the best storyteller of them all.

Coach has often left Karankawa County in disgust, but always returned. "Because it holds a kind of grim fascination for me," he says. "I can't seem to stay away for long."

He's been retired for several years now, and looks older than he is. The seams in his face deepen with each passing year, and his brow furrows as he speaks of Karankawa County from the deck of his ranch house near Janus Point.

Though repeated by others, these are all his stories; the most personal of which were won through unmitigated bribery. The ultimate bribe being Scotch whiskey and a willing ear.

Maud and Mahatma

Maud bought the Country Tavern in the middle 1960s, right after the Crime Commission declared it had chased all the prostitutes out of Karankawa County, shut down the houses, and got the high sheriff fired. Maud was a practical woman and didn't waste time with self-pity when the Crime Commission acted. At first, for a few days after all her friends were kicked out on the street, she felt sorry for them. She had a sweet and forgiving nature and a strong streak of the humanitarian, despite her chosen profession, and her solicitude was deep. But after giving it much thought, she knew the Crime Commission hadn't succeeded.

"Each of you find one of those nice residential areas and buy you a house," Maud told the other women. "Act respectable. Then turn all the tricks you want to, right in the comfort of your own home."

Most of them did as Maud suggested. In some cases it was necessary for two or three to assume a mortgage together, but many of them succeeded. And their success only confirmed their respect for Maud's logic. Thus the Crime Commission spread prostitution into all the restricted and tree-shaded neighborhoods of Karankawa County, Texas.

Afterwards, on cool mornings before the sun rose too high for comfort, Karankawa County whores drank coffee on quiet patios with unsuspecting housewives. They listened to the wives complain about husbands, kids, and dishwashers, and they nodded and frowned in deep commiseration over complaints about inattentive spouses. And on the first day of each month, they deposited zippered bags full of tax-free cash in Karankawa County banks.

Maud's friends' new respectability and prosperity made them

happy, and every time they thought of Maud they were thankful for her college education and experience as an English teacher. They were sure it was Maud's background that had solved their problem.

Janus Point, Texas, sits on the Gulf of Mexico across the ship channel from Louisiana. When Maud bought the Country Tavern, the highway sign on the edge of town said, "Janus Point Pop. 963."

North and west of Janus Point stretches a great salt marsh, south is the Gulf, and one could almost throw a rock—if there were any rocks—eastward and hit the Louisiana shore of the ship channel. Large, flat-decked workboats move up and down the channel, nursing the city of offshore platforms in the Gulf. Stately, quiet, and slow-moving tankers glide past Janus Point. Flocks of seabirds follow the ships, and helicopters fly back and forth from the Gulf making crew changes on oil rigs. Gulf Coast ranchers drive through the town pulling cattle trailers loaded with cows, horses, and yelping cur-dogs. Shrimpers, smelling of fish, wearing shin-high, white rubber boots and wind-roughened faces, dock their boats in the muddy channel, sell their catch, and hurry to one of two beer joints for rest and relaxation.

"You can't just *happen on* Janus Point," Maud often said, "you gotta be goin' there on purpose."

After Maud had been in Janus Point eleven years, the sign outside town said, "Janus Point Pop. 879."

The town had lost 84 people.

Some died, many moved out, and nobody moved in—except Mahatma and the High Plains Drifter. But Maud was sure they would never be counted in the census.

Janus Point natives, generally the descendants of families who had lived there more than a hundred years, were puzzled, though not overly concerned, about the town's lack of growth. They watched the ships pass, saw the choppers fly to and from the Gulf, and wondered why none of those engaged in the frantic offshore activity ever settled in Janus Point. The Janusians left their ramshackle homes daily, drove past porches and yards cluttered with rusting old boats, washing machines, ancient refrigerators, and the carcasses of worn-out cars, and saw nothing amiss. They didn't smell the open sewers

9

or the putrid fish from the docks; they shrugged at the ignorance of those who lived somewhere other than Janus Point, and went happily about their business. To them it was inconceivable that anyone could dislike their town. And when hurricanes threatened, they pointed out how every place on earth is subject to *some* sort of natural disaster.

In summer Janus Point is a watering place for sun and sand seekers who head for its beaches. There are visitors from Karankawa City, Beaumont, Houston, Dallas, and even far-away places like Minnesota and Illinois. Some Janus Point merchants believe the town could be a real tourist attraction with a little advertising and cleaning up.

But most of the old-line Janusians don't get excited about that. They take their time, drink their beer, and watch it all go past.

Mahatma arrived in Janus Point in the summer of 1981, several years after the Arabs taught Texas oil people just what dealing was all about. Nobody knew Mahatma's real name because nobody asked, and Mahatma never offered to tell. But Maud knew he had come to Janus Point hot and hungry with $1.26 in the pocket of his fatigues, his shoe soles flopping, an army-green T-shirt tied around his waist, and cold beer on his mind. His face was beet red and showing blisters, and graying auburn hair hung in a ragged mass from his head when he limped into the Country Tavern.

Maud stood tall, cool, beautiful, and grinning behind the bar of her establishment and watched as he flopped on a bar stool and crossed his legs yoga fashion. She got a frosty mug, filled it with draft beer, and silently handed it to Mahatma.

He blew the foam off the beer and drank it all down without taking it from his lips. "Thank you ma'am," Mahatma said as he set the mug down, reached into his pocket, and placed the $1.26 on the bar. "I hope this is enough money."

Maud shook her head. "That one's on the house. The rest will be six bits apiece."

"Then I'll have one more," Mahatma grinned.

"Looks like you've worn out your shoes." Maud watched Mahatma sip the second mug of beer.

"Looks like," he nodded and reached to rub his sore feet.

Maud was not without experience in sizing up the character of men. Her eyes were sharp; not one detail of Mahatma's appearance and demeanor escaped her. His accent told her he was from the South. Not Texas though, she thought; maybe Arkansas or Tennessee. His easy manner and direct gaze intimated that he was comparatively honest, but she saw some conflict in that. He wasn't used to the sun, he blistered easily, and his fatigues and army-green told her something else: unless he had bought them at G.I. Surplus, he was an army man. Her mind jumped ahead of her mental notes, and she made what she regarded as a logical conclusion: federal prison.

"What was you in for?" Maud bluntly asked.

He raised his blue eyes slowly and looked at her. "Is it still that plain?"

"It is to me," Maud answered, "but then I'm not a real average bear."

"Manslaughter," Mahatma said. "Shot an officer in 'Nam."

"Did he need killin'?"

"Yes'm," Mahatma solemnly nodded, "he needed killin'."

Maud took his empty mug and refilled it. "When you finish the beer, you can get that mop and broom in the corner and start cleaning. Then when you finish that, take this garbage out back while I make you some hamburgers."

"Yes'm," Mahatma said.

And so it was that Mahatma went to work in Janus Point, Texas, at the Country Tavern for Maud.

Five months later, the High Plains Drifter drove into Janus Point from Amarillo in a '65 Chevrolet pickup truck. It was December, and the air had a nip in it when he parked in front of the Country Tavern and swaggered in. He wore a high-crowned, flat-brim, western hat with a rattlesnakeskin band that had seven of the snake's rattles hanging from it. The rattles hung from the back of the hat and rustled softly when the Drifter moved about. He sported a fringed deerskin jacket, blue jeans and high-topped cowboy boots.

The fringed jacket was buttoned to the Drifter's throat. His beard was black and flecked with gray, and a ragged scar ran from below his right eye into the beard. His eyes were blue and cold.

Maud smiled, shook the cascade of frosted hair that framed the classic lines of her face and fell loosely about her shoulders, then watched the Drifter take off his coat. She saw a heavy bowie knife sheathed at his side.

"Whiskey!" the Drifter demanded as he rubbed his hands briskly against the cold and sat down.

"Gettin' cold, isn't it?" Maud served him the cheapest whiskey she had. "That'll be one-seventy-five."

He pulled a large roll of ones from his pocket, peeled off two, and handed them to her. "Keep the change," the Drifter said pompously.

"Damn," grinned Maud, "you mean this whole quarter?"

Her facetiousness was lost on him. He waved his hand to show his complete indifference. "Money don't mean nothing to me."

Maud put the bills in the cash register and slipped the quarter into her apron pocket. She had looked the Drifter over carefully, noted the scuffed and worn cowboy boots, seen two rips in the deerskin jacket where it lay on the table behind him, and appraised the frayed collar of his plaid shirt. She looked at his hands and saw they were soft, comparatively clean, without callouses, and scarless. Here, decided Maud, is a man who has never worked in his life.

"Lookin' for a job?" Maud asked.

He snorted and coughed. "I got money, don't need no job." He drank the whiskey down in two gulps.

He's a remittance man, Maud thought. A by-God-modern-day-remittance-man. She didn't bother to ask him, she was certain of it. And the bowie knife, she figured, showed the man was afraid . . . maybe a coward.

"Is there a hotel here in this jerkwater?" the Drifter asked.

Maud nodded southward. "Boarding house, Mrs. Alfred's. It's all we have."

The Drifter put on his coat and left.

And so it was that the High Plains Drifter moved into Mrs. Alfred's boarding house in Janus Point, Texas.

That first night at the Country Tavern, Mahatma slept on Maud's pool table.

"You can't sleep outside, you don't have any money, and you damned sure aren't gonna sleep with me," Maud explained. "So that leaves the pool table. I don't think you're a thief, but if you are, you're wasting your time—there's nothing here to steal. Besides, there's only one road out of here and you would get caught easily. Goodnight. We'll talk more in the morning."

Maud retired to her quarters on the second floor above the Country Tavern, while Mahatma, already stretched out on the pool table, watched the slow rhythm of her hips as she ascended the stairs. He wondered how it would have been to go with her. But, even had he known of her previous profession, he couldn't have known she had remained chaste and pure since her forced retirement by the Crime Commission.

The next morning, after she had fed him a hamburger for breakfast, Maud bought a razor and shaving cream at the small grocery down the street from the Country Tavern. She handed them to him. "Shave that ragged face," she said. "You look pitiful."

He took the shaving equipment and started toward the men's room, then turned and asked, "You got any scissors I could use for a few minutes? I need to cut this hair."

Maud nodded firmly, "You shave, *I'll* cut your hair."

Mahatma was immediately convinced she had barbered for years.

But Maud proved inept at barbering. When she finished clipping, Mahatma looked at his uneven, butchered hair and decided it had looked better before she touched it. He cursed softly as he appraised himself in the mirror behind the bar.

"Well," Maud shook her head, "maybe you should have cut it after all."

He stalked to the men's room, lathered his head with shaving cream, and shaved it smooth as his cheeks. He rolled up the legs of the army fatigues to his knees, hung the green T-shirt on the lavatory, grabbed a bar of soap, slipped out the back door of the Country Tavern, and started toward the river channel a few hundred yards away. His shoe soles flopped as he walked; curled back under his feet and caused him to stumble.

"Shit!" Mahatma said. And he sat down on the oyster-shell path, took the shoes off and, still sitting, threw them as far into the tall weeds beside the path as he could.

He limped toward the channel. The oyster shells hurt his feet even though he placed each step carefully, but he persevered with gritted teeth and reached the edge. He stepped gingerly into the water, felt the warm mud ooze between his toes, waded out a few steps, and began soaping himself.

He felt better when he had finished. He had slipped dripping and unseen through the door and already sat, yoga fashion, barefoot and shirtless with shaved head, before Maud turned and saw him.

"Jesus Christ!" She peered at him closely. "You've *skinned* yourself! Look at you . . . all you need is one of those little spinnin' wheels . . . you look just like Mahatma Gandhi!"

From that moment, he was known in Janus Point, Texas, as Mahatma.

It was a week after Maud christened him, a week during which she called the name, "Mahatma," whenever she needed him for some odd job, that he finally asked: "Who the hell is Mahatma Gandhi!"

Maud was delighted. The latent school teacher in her responded and she ran up the stairs to her quarters and returned with a book.

"Here," she handed him the book, "read this."

He looked at the book's cover. It was a Gandhi biography. He riffled through the pages. "Uh-h-h, sometimes I don't read so good."

"Don't worry about it, I'll help you if you get stuck."

Mahatma spent a month laboriously reading the Gandhi book. Each night after Maud closed the Country Tavern, he stretched out and read by the huge double lights over the pool table.

It was the first time he had ever read a whole book.

He slept on the pool table, Maud fed him, let him drink moderate amounts of beer, and kept him busy cleaning, painting, and doing small repairs the Country Tavern had needed for a long time. She couldn't pay him, and he walked around broke, barefoot, and shirtless. His feet toughened until he could walk to the river for his bath with scarcely a limp, his skin tanned, and he began shaving his head every few days.

"Because it feels cleaner," he told Maud.

But that was not the whole truth.

For during that month, somewhere inside Mahatma, like building blocks along the edges of his semiliterate mind, a perverted vanity was slowly being erected. He was proud of the name she had given him, and he shaved his head so he would look like Gandhi. The name gave him an identity he had never experienced. In the

Arkansas orphanage he had been just another orphan; in the army, only a soldier; and in prison he had been treated as a complete non-entity. But here, in Janus Point, Texas, he was suddenly *somebody*.

He was Mahatma of the half-naked body and shaved head, who sat with legs crossed in the lotus position, balanced on bar stools, and meditated.

He practiced looking like Gandhi.

One morning, after his bath in the muddy ship channel, Mahatma told Maud he was moving out. "I found me a place to live," he said.

"Well, I'll miss you," Maud answered, "but I don't blame anyone for not wanting to sleep on a slate-topped pool table."

He moved into an old, yellow school bus someone had dragged into the salt marsh and abandoned. It had neither engine nor wheels, but its doors and windows worked and its seats were intact. Mahatma slept on the long seat at the rear of the bus and cooked on a Sears barbecue he had rescued from the roadside.

The bus was almost invisible from the shell road that ran next to the marsh. Tall marsh cane grew all around it, and the cane tops waved higher than the bus in the south wind. Whenever Mahatma trotted half-naked down the footpath through the tall cane to his school bus home at twilight, he was reminded of Southeast Asia. The incoming helicopters from the Gulf, flying across the great marsh as they brought work crews back to the shore, added to the Asian illusion and filled the air with their chopping sound until darkness fell. After dark the high hum of mosquito swarms replaced the sound of the helicopters. Mahatma lighted chemical incense to ward off the mosquitoes and burned candles to read.

And sometimes, in moments between late daylight and early darkness, he remembered the dead children . . .

They were scattered about the Vietnamese village, broken and bleeding, dead and dying, some moaning and softly crying, some quiet in eternal silence as the captain continued to spray them with gunfire. He watched himself raise the rifle, again felt his finger tighten on the trigger, and saw the captain's head transformed into a bright red, blossoming flower . . .

He got a job as a deckhand on a shrimp boat, worked for three weeks at sea, and found, upon his return, that he was rich enough to live a few months without working at all. He bought several bottles of gin and a few groceries. He stayed drunk till his money and gin ran out—he never worried much about the groceries—then went back to work.

And, drunk or sober, he practiced being Mahatma. He sat with legs crossed on bar stools and drank gin. His attitude was meditative, his face impassive, and strangers to the Country Tavern were likely to glance at him nervously from their eye-corners as he sat half-naked, arms folded across his bare chest, and stared at a spot on the wall. He often unnerved tourists. Many of them left after one drink.

"Why do you allow him to scare off paying customers?" asked Consuela, one of Maud's associates of pre–Crime Commission times.

Maud shook her head and smiled. "Well, it means an awful lot to Mahatma to *be Mahatma*. See, he's working his show. You ever think how important that is—just being able to work your own show? I guess I let him alone because it's so important to him."

Consuela knitted her brow and drew herself up to her full five feet, two inches. She took a deep breath and her breasts rose before her magnificently, their size emphasized by her slight form; she was conscious of the impression she made. "But don't he cost you money?"

"Probably," Maud shrugged. "But not much. There aren't many tourists anyway, and once in a while I'll see one who's been here before pointing at Mahatma and collecting money from someone he's brought along. Like he just won a bet."

Consuela shivered and watched Mahatma stare at the wall. "He gives me goosebumps. I see in his face long silences and empty miles. He has a kinship to great, desolate distances, I think."

"He would be tickled to hear that," Maud laughed. "That's what he would like you to think. He's workin' his show on you."

"Hey, hombre!" Consuela yelled at Mahatma, "you're far out!"

Mahatma stared unblinking at the wall and didn't answer. He was too busy working his show.

In the months before the Drifter's December arrival in Janus Point, Mahatma's reading led to more reading, which created questions in his mind and led to even more reading, until he thought his head would burst from study. Gandhi, Mahatma learned, was very much affected by Henry David Thoreau, and Mahatma hadn't the slightest idea who Thoreau was. So he asked Maud, who remained a closet school teacher despite all she could do to overcome it. She still "squandered her money on books," according to friends like Consuela.

"Get your hair fixed, buy some new clothes," Consuela often told her. "Why spend good money on books?"

But Maud had always bought books, so when Mahatma asked about Thoreau, all she had to do was run upstairs and bring back copies of *Walden* and *Civil Disobedience*.

"See?" Maud told a skeptical Consuela as they watched Mahatma leave the Country Tavern with the Thoreau volumes. "That's a good reason for buying books. Hell, just knowing Mahatma's the least bit interested in Thoreau—well, it makes me feel sorta like Billy Graham."

Consuela looked puzzled. "Who is Billy Graham?"

"Well," said Maud, "I can run upstairs, I've got a book on him . . ."

"Never mind," Consuela said quickly, "I got to go anyway, I've got this appointment."

Mahatma struggled through the Thoreau books. He was impressed and began to memorize the most quotable Thoreau passages. He ran them over and over in his mind as he stared at the wall in the Country Tavern, thought about them as he graded shrimp, and read them by candlelight in the yellow school bus. He was contemplating Thoreau when he first met the Drifter in the Country Tavern.

It was a few days after the Drifter had settled into Mrs. Alfred's boardinghouse that he came stomping and scowling into Maud's Country Tavern, ordered himself a whiskey while he waited for his eyes to adjust to the dim light, then spotted Mahatma meditating several bar stools away.

"Damn," the Drifter said to Maud, inclining his head toward Mahatma, "what is that?"

"That's Mahatma," Maud answered, "he works here sometimes."

"He looks like he needs wormin'," the Drifter said, then turned sideways to Mahatma could see the big bowie knife at his hip. "Where's his shoes?"

"He don't wear shoes," Maud told the Drifter, "when he's meditatin'."

"Well I been to six rodeos and some goat ropin's," laughed the Drifter, "but I ain't never seen nothin' quite like him."

Having heard the whole exchange, and without moving from his yoga position, Mahatma quoted Thoreau as closely as he could remember. "*Better you had been born in a cow lot and suckled by a bitch coyote.*"

Inaccurate though it was, Maud was impressed beyond the telling and once more felt the rapture of an evangelist.

The Drifter, however, was incredulous and incensed. "What did you say about my mama?" he screamed, pulling the bowie knife from its sheath and starting toward Mahatma.

But Mahatma, violently, without thought and more quickly than the Drifter could believe, wheeled about on the revolving barstool and with one fluid and sweeping motion, grabbed up a heavy metal chair and broke the Drifter's knife arm just above the wrist. The bowie knife clattered to the floor, Maud gasped, the Drifter clutched his broken arm with his other hand, and Mahatma quietly returned to his lotus position.

Tears ran down the Drifter's rough cheeks. "My God, he broke my goddamned arm! My knife arm too! What am I gonna do now?"

"*The mass of men,*" Mahatma gently quoted, "*lead lives of quiet desperation.*"

After he and Maud had taken the Drifter, in his own truck, to the doctor and got the arm set, Mahatma was firmly lectured by Maud as the three of them sat in the Country Tavern.

"Passive resistance?" Maud shamed him. "Nonviolence? Your thinking isn't very consistent when you run around quoting Thoreau and breaking arms."

"*Nonviolence is better than violence,*" Mahatma quoted, "*but violence is better than cowardice.*"

"But I wasn't gonna cut you, I just wanted you to *think* I was." The Drifter was still upset, sobbing pitifully and in a state of near shock. The rattlesnake rattles shook with his crying. "I ain't never cut nobody in my whole life."

It was true. The Drifter feared and hated violence, and because of that abhorrence he looked upon himself as a failure. Indeed, he had felt so since he'd been four years old, when his father, the owner of an immense ranch in the Texas Panhandle, had put him upon the back of a gentle pony. The Drifter had screamed in terror and his father had called him, "sissy."

He grew up on the ranch with violence all around him. Ripping, running horses and cattle, shouting men, the smell of burning hair at branding time and the sight of blood when calves were castrated ... he hated all of it.

His father pushed him into high school sports, where he received the scar but failed again. He grew the beard, sported the rough dress of a working cowboy, and acted tough; but none of it worked. He was a gentle man and his father despised him for it. The old man was relieved when the Drifter left the ranch, happy to send the monthly checks wherever his son happened to be.

"I forgive you," Mahatma said, "and I'm sorry about your arm."

"Maybe," Maud told the Drifter, "you could wear the knife on your left side, since you're not gonna cut anybody—since you're just wearing it for show." Maud knew the knife was important to the Drifter.

So he wore the bowie knife on his left side till his arm healed, and Maud and Mahatma never divulged how his arm had been broken nor how he had cried about it like a child.

It was in that manner that the Drifter and Mahatma became fast friends, and it came to pass that they worked their show together in the Country Tavern under the auspices of Maud the whore.

Mahatma would strike his yoga pose and meditate, while the Drifter sat nearby, picked his teeth with the big knife, and looked ominous. And when a customer of Maud's asked a question or commented on the economy, government, or social conditions, Mahatma would mouth a Thoreau-ism only vaguely related to the topic. But, regardless of how inept his statement, or how inappropriate, his dress and demeanor suggested wisdom. He seemed so sure of himself, spoke so evenly, clearly, and without hesitation, that most people were fascinated.

And for those who doubted Mahatma's veracity, there was always the Drifter who sat fingering his bowie knife. He looked vicious, so people never asked Mahatma deeply probing questions. Besides, Maud was the only one in the Country Tavern who could recognize the mild deception, and she saw no harm in it — even after the rumor started.

The rumor was begun by a refugee from Detroit who had come to Janus Point to escape Michigan snow and unemployment. He was successful in escaping the snow, but Southeast Texas was deep in the throes of oil recession, and unemployment was just as rampant there.

"The Drifter is Mahatma's bodyguard," the Detroit man whispered to a friend, "and Mahatma is a graduate of Columbia, Harvard, and a Zen master besides. Look at the scar on the Drifter's face. Look at those cold eyes. Why, he would as soon kill you as look at you. And he's devoted to Mahatma. See that cast on his arm? He got that arm broken defending Mahatma from a whole motorcycle gang."

When the captain of the shrimp boat where Mahatma worked heard the story, he yelled, "Horseshit! He's a damned Arkansas ridge runner, and dumb as a day-old baby. I'll swear, we're guardin' the wrong damned border." The captain nodded toward the Red River in distant north Texas. "We need to build a fence up yonder instead of the Rio Grande. Keep some of them dam-yankees out."

But the story remained. And it made its rounds in Janus Point until most people came to think it was true. For it was the sort of story people wanted to accept; somehow it made them feel better to believe there was one in their midst who had quick, simple answers to complex questions.

Maud only nodded when Consuela told her about the story spreading. She shrugged and told Consuela it made no difference.

Maud had long ago decided life narrows down on you. She couldn't explain it well, but she believed life changed from your own super highway, when you're young, to a thin neck of a footpath when you're old. So, she thought, if it made Mahatma and the Drifter happy to work their show, and if folks wanted to believe Mahatma was some kind of prophet, she was willing to let them.

Despite her abundance of self-confidence, Maud was overcome by the country surrounding Janus Point. It seemed to her the tiny town would be difficult for an artist to paint. There was entirely too much green marsh and too much blue — both sea and sky — and not enough town. She was awed by her sense of wind, sea, sky, and sun . . . it was unbalancing to her. And her mind often sniffed at a thinly covered savagery in the land. A quiet but ever threatening violence hung over it, she thought, and embraced it like a fog from the Gulf of Mexico. She shivered whenever that mist of violence touched her consciousness, and she was afraid.

In her mind was an irrational image of Janus Point. At the bottom center of the United States, wedged between the North American continent and the Gulf of Mexico, it seemed to her to have a magnetism all its own. She could see, in her mind, how human flotsam – herself, Mahatma, the Drifter, Consuela, and others – had tumbled southward, downward, to lodge in Janus Point like uprooted trees in a spring flood. She often thought in images rather than words, and the image of human wreckage falling into Janus Point, inexorably, helplessly, was persistent in her mind, and unsettling.

She saw Mahatma as a stabilizing influence to those hapless bits of humanity, and she hoped he would give them something to hold to, something worthy from his reading and study.

By 1984, after three years in Janus Point, Mahatma had come to spend an inordinate amount of time reading, studying, and discussing ideas with Maud. His reading tastes broadened and his acting ability improved; he practiced voice and timing, and he bought a pair of steel-rimmed glasses and some worn sandals to enhance his Gandhi role. And whenever he wasn't reading, he sat in the Country Tavern with the Drifter beside him and worked his show. He no longer had to work on the shrimp boat; people began to leave donations for him with the Drifter. It was not uncommon for Mahatma, at the end of a busy night at the Country Tavern, to earn as much as fifty dollars. It was more than he needed. He continued to live in the school bus, ate little, and his patrons paid for his gin at the Country Tavern.

He became such an attraction that Maud had a small "temple," as she called it, built for him inside the beer joint. Constructed in an oval shape with sheer cloth curtains for walls, and a sumptuous red couch on which Mahatma sat and held forth, it looked more like a cathouse bedroom. But the patrons were nonetheless impressed, and they sat in attentive clusters around Mahatma's feet, asked questions, and drank large amounts of Maud's liquor until closing time each night.

And for a long time Mahatma, Maud, and the Drifter were happy playing their Janus Point roles, working their own show. But discord and dissension slipped up on them unseen and unheard.

Perhaps it was blown in by the breeze off the Gulf; or maybe it came about through Mahatma's study, through words thick, lush, and packed together in his mind. Maybe, like other natural ironies, disharmony was born of Mahatma's thinking and meditation while he lay in the yellow school bus and listened to the rain play a golden melody on the marsh grass. It could have come from an eerie restlessness, a pushing, an urging. But it came. It came in the same way a power hunger is often born of love for country, the way evangelists change a search for God to a search for gold, and it was unseen and unexplained.

It was first felt by Snake Cormier.

Snake Cormier owned Snake's Rue Rouge in Janus Point. From where he lived Snake could hear the surf breaking on the beach, and on his morning walk to the Rue Rouge most of Janus Point was visible to him. The early sun slanted onto Snake's face, illuminated its long angles, his pockmarked cheeks, the thin tight mouth, and his small, close-set eyes that darted and shifted quickly, glancing about but never quite focusing. Snake's eyes licked at an object then slid away to lick at another, not ever tasting anything.

He looked at, but did not see, the muddy, oil-slick water in the ditch beside the shell road as he walked. It flowed in tiny swirls and ripples, rushed oblivious of its filth with the outgoing Gulf tide. He didn't focus on the half-submerged Lone Star beer bottle, the red and white plastic milk carton, or the condom floating in the brown water like a dead, white jellyfish. Across the ditch to Snake's left, a barbed wire fence sagged three rusty strands into tall marsh grass, and the marsh stretched wetly into the horizon as far as Snake could have seen . . . if he had looked.

A half-mile to the east, past more marsh grass and another shelled road, past Cleo's junkyard with its ugly acres of Ford, Buick, Cadillac, and Chevrolet skeletons, ran the river. Seventeen offshore drilling rigs stood idle on the channel's near side. Their tall derricks and jacked-up tripod legs, the long arms of silent draglines, the squat buildings that sat atop rig decks, and the various cables and pipes strung at odd angles, were silhouetted against the rising sun like mute testimonials to Southeast Texas' recession and a dying oil economy.

Halfway to the channel, hidden in cane, stood Mahatma's school bus.

An oil tanker filled with OPEC oil made its way slowly up the river, and in the distance a foghorn's sad bellow sounded. Behind Snake a fog bank moved across the Gulf toward the beach, quietly enveloped Snake's home in mist, then stalled and waited for the sun to melt it into the wet-hot Janus Point morning.

His bar, Snake's Rue Rouge, served beer, barbecue, and beans. Snake also sold bait—frozen shrimp and live minnows—and as far as Snake was concerned, he was in direct competition with Maud's Country Tavern. Snake's establishment was located on Janus Avenue, the main thoroughfare, and its brick facade sported two large windows, tall double doors with glass panes, and a neon sign which hadn't worked for years.

The sign read: SNAKE'S RUE ROUGE, BEER, BAIT, BEANS. But it could only be seen clearly in daylight on fogless days.

Before it exhausted its neon, the sign had spelled out its message in flashing green and yellow lights. Snake had ordered the sign in green and gold, the school colors of Janus Point, but what should have been gold was a faded yellow the first time electricity ignited the neon.

Snake raised hell about it, but the sign man stood firm and stoutly maintained that the yellow *was* gold. In the end, Snake even convinced himself it was indeed gold. In the years the sign had worked, flashing Snake's name in green and yellow, Snake convinced his hardhat customers it was green and gold.

Snake wasn't concerned with the sign's color or condition as he walked to work. He was concerned that he was slowly going broke. People were out of work in Karankawa County, and fewer of them could afford his beer, bait, and beans. But he was quite certain his misfortune was the fault of Maud's Country Tavern, not the economy.

Ronald Reagan was Snake's hero, as were all the proponents of free enterprise—including the oil companies busily engaged in laying off his customers—and, in Snake's mind, it would have been unpatriotic for him to blame the economy. He had, for the early part of the Reagan administration, maintained: "Businesses all fail for the same reason—poor management." But that was wearing a little thin. After all, to hold to that argument was to blame himself, and he could not, of course, bear that. So he blamed Maud and Mahatma.

One part of Snake questioned how Janus Point tolerated an ex-whore as part of the business establishment. He resented that and thought it somehow unclean. But he could never bring himself to vocalize that feeling because every time he visited the Country Tavern to scout his competition, he looked at Maud and felt a great stirring in his loins. Therefore, Snake Cormier was a tortured man who squirmed beneath the soft smile of Maud and suffered in unaccustomed silence.

He lusted after Maud in his heart, had fantasies about trysts in the moonlight, and could not bring himself to criticize her openly.

And he paid for it at home.

Snake's wife, Estelline of the shrill voice and cutting tongue, had no such hesitancy about Maud. "A common whore is putting you out of business," Estelline whined to Snake several times a week. "Starving your children . . . your wife."

On those occasions Snake eyed his fat wife carefully, trying to detect concrete evidence of her starving. And he once asked her, "What is the difference, Estelline, between a common and uncommon whore?"

"Don't be cute, Cormier," Estelline coldly told Snake, "or I'll knock fire from your ass."

And he knew she would. His wife outweighed him by some eighty-two pounds. She had, on several occasions when he had come home drunk, knocked him full out on the floor.

So Snake Cormier became a man in torment who spent his days watching through the windows of an almost vacant Rue Rouge as a steady stream of people entered and left Maud's Country Tavern. His pride suffered. And in time he came to believe his problem didn't stem from Maud, but from the growing popularity of Mahatma.

Maud noticed that the questions people asked Mahatma were repetitive, and she eventually learned to predict both the questions and Mahatma's answers.

24

Unemployed Yankees always wanted to know how they were going to make it without a job.

"*A man's wealth,*" Mahatma usually answered them, "*can be measured in direct proportion to what he can do without.*"

Those who came to the Country Tavern regularly would nod gravely at answers they had heard before, and newcomers were thunderstruck by Mahatma's sagacity and the clearness and simplicity of his answers.

And Maud, serving more drinks and making more money than since she had quit whoring, couldn't help it that the English teacher part of her was appalled. She wondered what would happen if she replaced Mahatma with a sign that simply said: READ!

She wondered what the reaction of the Country Tavern's customers would be. But she knew most people would never believe her; none of them would begin reading for answers. It was easier and more fun to listen to Mahatma, then run home and tell about a mystic one had met in a Janus Point beer joint.

But Snake Cormier, as he sat one night in the Country Tavern, drunk, having closed down the Rue Rouge early after mentally telling Estelline to go to hell, listened to Mahatma, and the glamour of it was somehow lost on him.

"How the hell," Snake drunkenly asked, as Mahatma sat in his temple and worked his show, "can you sit there and claim to be so damned *good* while you're starvin' my kids?"

"Ease up some, Snake," Maud quickly answered him, "you're way outa line."

Snake got up, properly chastened, and staggered out of the Country Tavern. He stumbled home and was met at the door by an irate Estelline who promptly decked him.

And as far as Maud was concerned, the incident was over.

But Mahatma saw it differently the next morning. "Do you reckon I'm hurtin' his business that much?" he asked Maud.

"I dunno," she shrugged. "Maybe you are at that."

So Mahatma walked the two blocks to Snake's Rue Rouge that very day, and it came to pass that he and the Drifter began to work their show at the Country Tavern and Snake's Rue Rouge on alternate nights. Estelline was happy with Snake because his business improved, Maud still profited, and Mahatma and the Drifter didn't care where they were, as long as they could drink and work their show.

Snake built Mahatma a "mosque" in the Rue Rouge, and Janus Point night life fell into a pattern that was quickly learned by the regulars and pointed out to visitors. Sometimes, when Mahatma was absent from Maud's or Snake's place, the proprietor would close down and go wherever Mahatma was. So, in Janus Point, Texas, unless Mahatma was present there was no night life.

And Maud felt settled in a routine until one night an asinine, dreamy-eyed young woman asked, "What is life all about?"

Maud smiled and wondered what Thoreau nugget Mahatma might toss her.

She was surprised when Mahatma answered, "Screwin' and fightin'."

"That's very crude," said the dreamy-eyed girl. "Surely you can do better than that."

"No," Mahatma gravely answered, "because it's the truth. It's basic."

Maud was shocked. The answer, as far as she could remember, was not from Thoreau. And even if such a thing had been said before, Maud was quite sure Mahatma had arrived at it alone. It was original.

"Name me most anything humans do," Mahatma explained, "and I'll show you it's related to sex or violence . . . sometimes both."

"God!" said the girl in obvious disgust.

"God is love," said Mahatma, "and love leads to screwin'."

The girl closed her eyes tightly and shook her head. "Jesus!"

"Same deal," Mahatma shrugged.

Maud and the Drifter sat and stared at Mahatma as the girl gathered up her purse and stormed out of the Country Tavern.

And Maud felt the first blush of an idea.

In the early summer of 1984, no one in Janus Point wondered who had called the television station. Channel 88 simply appeared one night at the Country Tavern and began unloading cameras, equipment, and lights from their van. Everyone recognized the van. It was red, white, and blue, and emblazoned upon its sides and roof was the logo—a huge, blue eyeball around which was written: THE SOUTHEAST TEXAS BIG EYE.

The fact that Maud had replaced some of the worn curtains of

Mahatma's throne with new ones; that she had purchased a new and more expensive couch upon which Mahatma lounged and spoke; and that she had, only a week before, completed a gleaming paint job on the Country Tavern's exterior, went unquestioned.

It was regarded as coincidental that Channel 88's Big Eye arrived on the night Maud sold bargain, two-for-one drinks, which ensured a large crowd. And nobody noticed the uncommon number of Maud's friends scattered about the Country Tavern that night; that those women asked Mahatma a great number of questions; nor that their questions seemed to be asked in a practiced manner.

On the contrary, the Country Tavern was filled with regulars when Channel 88 arrived, and they were not in the least surprised by the taping. For afterward, when the memorable night was done, they assured each other that they had long wondered when such a thing would happen.

"After all," one of them asserted, "you can't keep brilliance under wraps forever."

The only person present who was surprised that night was Maud. She was both surprised and delighted, and for the first time she felt a faint stirring inside herself for Mahatma.

It was after the whores planted about the room had asked their practiced questions, the answers to which Maud easily predicted, that a young man with a northern accent asked Mahatma, "What's wrong with this country? What's wrong with America?"

The place was quiet except for the tinkling of glasses and the soft whirring of ceiling fans. Blue cigarette smoke was pulled upward by the fans and dissipated, and people waited for Mahatma's answer as he shifted his position on the couch, adjusted his steel-rimmed glasses, and finally spoke.

"America," Mahatma said in his practiced tone, "is still fragmented into social, economic, and cultural groups with hardset boundaries. Our people are generally too quick to say, 'Look who I am, what I own, where I live. See my title? I'm more important than you because of these things I own.'"

Feeling the television cameras on him, he formed his words carefully and worded a longer answer than was his custom.

"Americans find it easy to lie. We have little depth and live with many fantasies and untruths. We often lie about our personal selves,

27

and we're alone because of it. We are too quick to change, we seem to believe change is inherently good . . . we accept and equate change with progress. We are narrow in the scope of our thinking—specialized—and we have few generalists, which probably means less broad understanding. We are too concerned with winning—to be first, we think, makes us a better human."

Mahatma looked levelly at the man who had asked the question and adjusted the glasses again. "We have a great many problems, most of which stem from greed."

Maud was stunned. Never, not in her wildest fantasies, would she have expected such an answer. Again, she was sure Mahatma had formulated his response as he spoke.

Somehow, as is often true with paintings, films, or taped television, the product of Channel 88's work looked better than the real thing. On television, the interior of the Country Tavern took on a golden glow, the curtains and couch of Mahatma's temple were softly enhanced by the glow, and Mahatma's features were shadowed subtly, so that his eyes seemed alternately hidden and shining. The overall effect suggested mystery, the occult, and a kind of sagacious inscrutability. And his voice, deep, profound, and practiced as that of a Mississippi preacher, appeared to captivate an audience whose faces showed rapt attention.

He was, after the Southeast Texas Big Eye had shone upon him with its huge, blue retina, an instant celebrity.

Perhaps, had Southeast Texas not been in a deep recession, and if many of its people hadn't been afraid, jobless, and casting about them for the merest shred of truth—or if enough of those fun-loving, beer-drinking, laughing, and for the most part non-reading people had been able to see through Mahatma—he would have been perceived only as a brief diversion.

But such was not the case.

Mahatma grasped, and held, the attention of Karankawa County and Southeast Texas.

Maud's Country Tavern enjoyed standing-room-only crowds after Mahatma's television appearance, and Snake's Rue Rouge was literally inundated with people on alternate nights. Estelline quit worrying about starvation, and on the nights Snake closed down and went to the Country Tavern, she even allowed her husband to come home drunk without punishment. While Snake, on those nights in the Country Tavern, sipped whiskey, stared at Maud, and fantasized, the Drifter sat and picked his teeth with the bowie knife.

And the spirit of Janus Point quickened.

There was a great clamor among Southeast Texans to see Mahatma and to hear the words of his mouth—words which seemed to leap cleanly from within him, each one filling the air with tiny explosions. Maud, practical, earthy, and without illusion, was herself occasionally caught up and swept along by his voice, and she was hard put to take hold and jerk herself back to reality.

She was reminded of another Southeast Texas phenomenon she had read about and seen on television, and she shivered at the memory.

There had been a celebrated screen door in the community of Little Abbeville; when the sunlight touched it at certain angles the door had reflected a perfect image of a popular artist's rendition of Jesus Christ.

Maud remembered how people had come from miles around, had knelt, fingered prayer beads, and worshiped before the screen door at the rear of the house in Little Abbeville. And she recalled how the good people who owned the house had had to set up schedules for the screen door's viewing; how the backyard grass had disappeared under the tramping of thousands of feet; how the leaves of the yard's shrubbery had vanished in the grasping fingers of worshipers until the bushes stood stark and denuded in the sun; and how the yard was finally reduced to bare dirt, dust hanging in the sunlit air.

People flocked to Janus Point the same way.

They arrived early in the afternoon to assure themselves a seat in the Country Tavern or Snake's Rue Rouge, and they stayed late. Janus Point merchants, being few in number and unaccustomed to such crowds, began to prosper. Those who had believed Janus Point could profit from the tourist trade reminded the unbelievers how they had predicted just such a thing. And the unbelievers nodded, grinned broadly, and totaled up their profits. Snake Cormier got his sign fixed, and it once more flashed his name in bright green and yellow. Storefronts were painted and repaired, the streets were kept neat and clean, and the old-line Janusians even began to take pride in their homes. They hauled the rusting old cars to the dump, removed wrecked refrigerators and ranges from front porches, and mowed weeds and grass until the community had a neat appearance.

In six weeks Janus Point was transformed.

Mahatma got little sleep. He insisted, even after acquiring celebrity status, on living in the yellow school bus. Nothing Maud could do or say dissuaded him, and although he viewed the world through a gin-soaked haze for many hours, he remained true to his Walden Pond philosophy.

"*Simplify, simplify, simplify,*" he quoted to Maud. "I'll not complicate my life with Things."

Maud stood in the doorway of his bus as she spoke. "But what if you get sick? What if something happens to you?"

He shook his head doggedly without answering. And Maud, hating herself for thinking it, was overwhelmingly conscious of an image, the image of the proverbial goose that laid the golden egg.

"Do you realize this whole town depends on your health?" she asked.

"I'm not moving."

She sadly looked around her. The crowds had also been to Mahatma's bus, and the cane was trampled down all about it. The marsh grass appeared in ragged patches where it had once been thick and ankle deep, and much of the area around the bus was bare, dark earth. Maud shrugged and walked away.

"Some of us march to a different drummer," Mahatma mumbled to himself as he watched the sway of her hips.

Who among us can truly explain matters of the heart?

Maud, experienced as any in love, was unable to explain away the sudden surge of feeling inside her. She who had remained chaste since leaving the whorehouse felt an unanticipated urge for Mahatma. She wanted him. But she could not be absolutely certain whether her desire was a pure yearning for Mahatma, the man, or if it was born of a desire to protect her investment. A child of her time, she was permeated to her very core with that teaching of her society which whispered to her, "Take care of your money first. . . ."

It was the thread of that whispering plaited together with strands of romantic love which confused her.

She did not trust herself.

Very much aware of her power over men—she knew, for example, how Snake watched her with lust in his heart—she had no doubt that she could seduce Mahatma. But, for the first time since she had been a teenager, she wanted more than seduction. The limited terms of seduction were not in the broad covenant she desired. She felt a proprietary interest in him, as if he were something she had created, and as such uniquely hers. But that feeling was accompanied by great billows of guilt that bathed her in self-loathing. For Maud was honest with herself about her feelings. The honesty was a practical thing, ensuring her against surprises which might materialize within her and cause her to stumble. And Maud was nothing if not practical.

She wrestled with her problem and became very angry with herself because of it. Hard as she had worked all her life, practicing against surprises from inside herself, she was nonetheless surprised.

And her anger became ugly. She snapped and snarled at those around her. She threw things—beer bottles, glasses, garbage cans—and she went about noisily kicking and rattling chairs and tables inside the Country Tavern. She became insufferable, and after two weeks people began to avoid her.

Except for Consuela, who looked at her through great brown pools of concern and asked, "You goin' through the change, or what?"

To which Maud retorted, "None of your damned business!"

"They must be locking you up and teasing you all night, then turning you loose on us every morning," said Consuela. "Goodbye. I'll see you when you're in a better mood."

But Consuela returned the very next day, and Maud, seeing Consuela's condition, was instantly contrite and concerned. For Consuela was almost hysterical, in tears, and her small hand was firmly gripped by a black child of ten. The little boy was crying too.

Gone was the anger as soon as Maud ran to embrace the bawling Consuela. Gone was the self-loathing as Maud knelt in front of the child and wiped away his tears with a bar towel. Quick as thought, Maud resumed being mother-comforter.

"This," said Consuela from behind her tears, "is Ahrah-si Jones."

"Ahrah-si?" asked Maud.

"Ahrah-si," Consuela nodded.

"Well what on earth is the matter?" Maud looked up at Consuela and kept wiping at Ahrah-si's face with the bar towel.

"I'm afraid they'll put him in the orphanage," Consuela blurted.

"But how . . . what . . ."

And Consuela explained.

In the way such things seem to be preordained by some malicious god, Ahrah-si's grandmother, his only known relative and Consuela's maid, had died. The grandmother had lived in Consuela's home for many years, and they had together delighted in rearing Ahrah-si from infancy.

Consuela bought his clothes, paid his doctor bills, and saw that he went to school and had everything he needed. So he became the child Consuela never had. She reveled in his growing up, and she had shared the joy with no one—not even her friend, Maud.

Consuela had not told her of the boy, she explained, for the same reason she was frightened now. She feared for Ahrah-si's future because she was herself an illegal alien, and even though she had lived in Texas for more than twenty years, the illegality hung over her every waking moment. She, like other Mexican nationals in Texas, moved about with fear and deep distrust of those in authority. She was certain someone would come to take Ahrah-si from her.

Maud shook her head, "No, Consuela, the authorities don't know Ahrah-si exists. They won't come and take him."

"But they will," Consuela cried. "I know they will, I can feel it in my bones. You must take him. I will pay . . . he can come here and live with you. I'll visit every day."

"He can't live here, Consuela," Maud told her firmly. "It wouldn't be right for him to live in a beer joint."

Ahrah-si had quit crying. He stood and listened without speaking. He looked at his bare feet while he traced large circles in the dust on the floor with his big toe.

Consuela turned to him. "Go outside, Ahrah-si. Look at the water, there are ships passing."

He ran out and started toward the channel.

"He can't live in this beer joint," Maud repeated.

"Como no?" Consuela shrugged and spread her fingers. "He already lives in a whorehouse."

Maud knew it was true. Consuela had three other women in her home.

"Please!" Consuela implored.

Maud sighed in defeat and looked up at the ceiling of the Country Tavern. "I'll make you a deal, Consuela. He can stay for a few days. Just until you can make other arrangements, understand; but that is absolutely all."

"You are an angel," Consuela hugged Maud tightly. "I knew you would help."

And so it was, in the summer of 1984, that Ahrah-si Jones came to live in the Country Tavern with Maud.

"He's black as a telephone, ain't he?" the Drifter said, flashing a grin so wide that the scar on his face crinkled and turned pink.

Maud knew the Drifter didn't mean to belittle or insult Ahrah-si; he was only stating a fact.

For Ahrah-si was the darkest person Maud had ever seen. He was also the most irrepressible. He bubbled over with mirth and good humor, he frolicked about like a happy pup, and to him life seemed no more than a daily, festive event. He filled the Country Tavern with activity in the early mornings, normally the time it was quietest, and he altered the life-styles of its people—Maud, Mahatma, and the Drifter—in ways they could not have imagined.

The Drifter loved him immediately, spent hours telling him stories of cowboys and cattle in West Texas, and let him closely examine the bowie knife. He carved Ahrah-si little figures of animals—cows, horses, bears—and wrapped them carefully in old newspaper and tied them with bright ribbons. He lay awake at night in his small room at Mrs. Alfred's boarding house thinking of Ahrah-si and new toys he could make for the boy.

Mahatma eyed the child nervously, conscious of his blackness and not quite knowing how to relate to him at first. But the innocence and enthusiasm natural to young children overcame that, and soon Mahatma began to take him fishing in the river several times a week. They often came in with a catch of flounder which Maud fried for the three of them. And they sat and ate lunch together in the Country Tavern like a happy family.

Maud, ever the schoolteacher, worked with Ahrah-si on his reading and writing skills. She read to him, had him read to her, and went to a bookstore in Karankawa City and happily bought armloads of books. To her unconcealed delight, she found his mind quick; he learned with alacrity.

Once when he was writing for her she told him, in the manner of a schoolteacher, "Put your name in the upper, left-hand corner, Ahrah-si."

He did, and when he finished the paper and gave it to her, the name appeared neatly in the correct place: R. C. Jones.

"But your name is R. C.," she squealed.

"Yes'm," he nodded, "that's my name, Ahrah-si."

"R. C.," she corrected.

"Ahrah-si," he repeated.

And Ahrah-si it remained.

Consuela came to visit every day, as she had promised, but she was unsuccessful in making "other arrangements" for the boy. The few days he was to spend became almost a month.

"I'm sorry," she apologized to Maud, "I just can't seem to work it out."

"I see," Maud told her in a noncommittal tone. For once more — the second time in less than a month — Maud was surprised by her feelings. She had come to hope Ahrah-si could stay with her indefinitely.

He had changed her life, and he had not, as she had at first feared, been any trouble. He split the long summer days between the Drifter, Mahatma, and herself. And at night, when the Country Tavern was busiest, he slept the deep and contented sleep of an exhausted child in his bed upstairs.

Besides, Maud thought while weighing, comparing, and dismissing her life's alternatives, Mahatma seemed to be closer to her because of the child. His usual reserve softened by Ahrah-si's happy countenance, Mahatma became less serious and concerned with his Walden philosophy. He laughed aloud at Ahrah-si, and sometimes,

34

when he wasn't aware of her, Maud saw him smiling softly as he watched the child at play.

And one day, inexplicably and naturally, in the way such things happen, Maud slipped her arm around Mahatma as they stood in perfect serenity and watched Ahrah-si fishing in the channel. And Mahatma turned and kissed Maud.

Within a week he abandoned the yellow school bus in the marsh and moved into the Country Tavern. And every night, after the place was closed, he lay beside Maud, and before sleep took him, he placed his hand upon the gently sloping curve where her hip became her waist, and he was content.

Maud was happy. She seemed to glow, Consuela noticed, with a new light. She smiled more, and her days were filled with caring for the child, Mahatma, and the Country Tavern.

"Mahatma," Consuela teased her, "seems to agree with you."

And though Consuela wasn't absolutely certain, she thought she saw Maud blush.

Two things happened in the week before Ahrah-si was to start school in Janus Point.

The first, they all thought, was fun. They watched, smiling fondly, as Ahrah-si unwrapped his newest present from the Drifter. When he got the paper off, Ahrah-si held the toy and examined it. Carved from the fork of an oak tree limb was a fine handgrip, and attached to the tips of the fork were two long strips of rubber, joined by a small leather pouch.

"What is it?" Ahrah-si asked with eyes shining.

"It's a slingshot," the Drifter proudly announced.

"How does it work?" Consuela frowned.

The Drifter took a handful of steel ballbearings from his pocket, retrieved the slingshot from Ahrah-si, and beckoned to them. "Come on outside, I'll show you."

Outside the Country Tavern, the Drifter fitted a ballbearing into the leather pouch, took aim at a post some thirty yards away, stretched the rubber strips, and let fly. The ballbearing struck the post with a satisfying "thwack!"

Ahrah-si ran to the post and examined the spot where the missile had struck. There was a deep indentation in the wooden post. "Gosh," said Ahrah-si Jones. "Ain't that some kinda fine?"

"Ain't that dangerous?" Consuela wanted to know.

"Naw," the Drifter assured her, "not if you don't shoot at people."

"You'll have to be careful with that thing," Mahatma warned Ahrah-si.

Ahrah-si nodded as the Drifter handed him a pocketful of ball-bearings, then ran off toward the ship channel to practice with his new toy.

The second thing happened two days later. Consuela was deported. The police, one of Consuela's "boarders" told Maud, raided the house and arrested them all. The others made bail, but Consuela, when it became obvious to the police that she was an illegal alien, was turned over to the immigration authorities.

"She's already gone," the sad woman told Maud. "By now she's in Mexico."

"She'll be back," Maud said comfortingly. "Before she even crosses the border, she'll start figuring how to return. You'll see."

Maud was certain that was the way of it, and the others bowed to her expertise in such matters.

"Consuela had to leave on a trip," Maud explained to Ahrah-si. "She'll be back in a few days."

Ahrah-si accepted her explanation, and they all went about their business. People continued to flock into Janus Point to see Mahatma, and the town prospered. Mahatma, always voracious for knowledge, was able to increase his study, and Maud helped him with books and whatever she could teach him.

He asked about mythology, and Maud answered by explaining the Roman deity for whom Janus Point was named. "He's a two-faced god, the god of beginnings. I think the gates of his shrine in the Roman Forum were only opened in time of war. His faces look both ways."

It was thus that Mahatma learned of contentment and mythological gods, and came to know that Janus Point was named for one of them.

It has been said that after one throws a pebble into the deep center of a pond, the pond will be forever changed. In the most subtle

way of change, in modes not readily discernible, ripples radiate out-
ward from the pebble's splash, gently wash the pond's banks, and
dislodge minute particles. Dirt, grass, seeds, tiny organisms, and de-
bris are washed into the water and the shoreline is changed. The
particles settle to the pond's bottom and its depth decreases infini-
tesimally. Perhaps, because of a pebble's splash, more food is washed
into the pond for resident fish, enabling one of them to live and
reproduce, so that eventually someone can eat that fish and survive. Who is to say?

In human affairs it is the same. Actions and words must radiate
out from the center in each of us, and, however tiny, their effect
must inevitably alter the world. How can it not be so?

It was such an idea that Mahatma was explaining from his throne
when the fight started in the Country Tavern. Even as he was speaking of immutable change, two men—neither of whom had known
in the morning that he would even be present in the Country Tavern that night—got into a fight. One called the other a "goddamned
redneck," and the other accused the first of being a "yankee sumbitch," and they fought.

Was it yet another battle in the Civil War?

Did it occur because Mahatma had appeared in Janus Point? Because of the dead children in Vietnam? Or because the man from
the north was in Janus Point looking for work? Was it because the
Japanese learned to make inexpensive cars, or because the local man
was jobless and drunk due to an increase in Arab understanding
of the oil business? Was it because Consuela was born to peonage
in Mexico, became a whore in Texas, loved a black child, and was
deported? Was it because the Karankawa Crime Commission closed
the whorehouses?

Regardless of the reasons, and there were thousands, the battle
was quickly joined and bloody.

Maud, forgetting Mahatma, Ahrah-si, and her personal safety,
and thinking only of how the violence might cause the Country
Tavern to be closed, stepped between the combatants, one of whom
began choking her. The man's eyes were glazed with a particular
madness, as if he cared little whom he choked, and he shook Maud
like a rag doll.

The Drifter, frightened by the violence and attempting to escape it, tried to run. He jumped to his feet, started across the room in front of Mahatma's curtained temple, and fell sprawling atop Mahatma's legs. The heavy bowie knife was in its place, within easy reach for Mahatma.

Ahrah-si, knowingly disobeying Maud's instructions about going to bed, was sitting on the stairs, watching. He held the slingshot and a steel ball bearing in his small hands, and he began screaming when the man started choking Maud. He put the ball bearing in the leather pouch, aimed, and shot at the man's head.

In almost the same instant, Mahatma pulled the big knife from the sheath, rolled the Drifter to the floor, stood, and threw the knife. His aim was good. The razor-sharp point of the bowie struck the man in the throat. It sliced through the jugular vein and the man began to choke on his own blood.

Ahrah-si's aim was not good. The steel ball hit Maud in the temple, and she fell dead upon the concrete floor of the Country Tavern.

The crowd stood frozen and quiet. The only sound was the Drifter's sobs. Ahrah-si ran upstairs and hid beneath Maud's bed. Mahatma returned to his couch, assumed his yoga pose, and ignored the two bodies on the floor.

The police arrived a few minutes later and handcuffed Mahatma. And as two of them led him toward the door of the Country Tavern — half-naked, shuffling along in his sandals, his small glasses on the end of his nose — Snake Cormier heard him say; "As the bowie knife flew through the air, I saw all the gods . . . Janus and all the rest. Janus had one face hidden in darkness, the other stared off into the distance. And I saw something else . . . *all* the gods have two faces."

The Drifter, Ahrah-si, and a Catholic priest attended Maud's funeral. They stood in September rain as her coffin was lowered into the marsh mud. Snake dressed that morning to go to the funeral, but Estelline threatened him with her accustomed vigor.

"After all, Cormier," Estelline said, "she was only a whore."

After the funeral, when the Drifter had loaded his truck and started back to Amarillo, he saw men boarding up the doors of the Country Tavern, and he watched as a State of Texas vehicle drove away with little Ahrah-si in the back seat. The Drifter cried as he headed the old truck northward, and his tears ran into his black beard.

Janus Point returned to normal. Within a month a citizen was seen moving a wrecked car into his front yeard, and soon old stoves and refrigerators began to appear on front porches. Trash gathered beside the highway and Snake Cormier's sign developed an electric short which he didn't bother to get fixed. Maud's books gathered dust in the Country Tavern. And even though the place was ransacked by looters, the books remained on the shelves untouched until fire claimed the building in February the following year.

The windows in Mahatma's bus were shattered and great holes were shot into its rusted-thin floor and roof from the inside, by duck-hunting teenagers trying out new shotguns. Winter rain blew in and rusted the floor of the bus, until great, gaping holes appeared. In the spring, sunlight slanted through the windows, shone down through the holes, and warmed the rich black earth around dormant cane. Green cane sprouts grew upward, thrust through the floor, and finally through the windows and roof.

By summer's end, tall cane waved in the south wind and the yellow bus was invisible.

War Hoss Kelly and the Brahma Bull

It was flat coastal land that stretched from the Gulf of Mexico to the Texas horizon. Squat trees with wind-twisted branches broke its monotonous sameness as if they had been haphazardly flung, like cast away cuttings from ancient forests, into lonely isolation in a sea of grass. It was an ugly land, and even though the trees were a soothing balm to Old Rip's eyes in the July heat as they fractured the level reach of grass, they were somehow foreign here. The trees didn't belong, and Old Rip loved and resented them at the same time. The ugly land sustained him, and the Gulf wind consoled him, and he understood the inner workings of this place.

He never told his grandson, W. H. Kelly, nor anyone else, but Old Rip Kelly was certain he observed miracles daily. He hand-pumped water every noon with an aging pitcher-pump—though he didn't have to; there were electric pumps on the ranch—and watched each gush of cool water as it splashed into the stock tank. It was hot work in Texas July heat, and he often let the cool water trickle through the calloused fingers of his left hand as he pumped with his right. The water gurgled upward with each sucking stroke, and Old Rip smiled inside himself as it burst sparkling and cold into the hot Texas sunlight. He was certain that every flowering of cool water was a tiny miracle.

In early mornings, surrounded by gleaming, dew-covered grass, Old Rip watched with feelings akin to awe while white Brahma calves drank breakfast from the teats of patient, cud-chewing mothers. The milk foamed whitely on the black mouths of fat calves, and he was convinced all this was miraculous too.

Old Rip had heard of men bargaining their souls away to the

40

devil. And, if he could have found the devil, he would happily have made that deal to keep this ranch. But the only devils he knew weren't interested in Old Rip's soul . . . they wanted his home.

It seemed a surety they would soon have it.

Two months before, on the night of W. H. Kelly's high school graduation, as the Karankawa High School Gator Band played "Pomp and Circumstance," Old Rip's heart had swelled with pride and quick tears had filled his hard blue eyes. He'd been impressed, and there weren't many things people did that impressed Old Rip.

He thought football, for example, was "damned foolishness and a waste of time." But he let W. H. play anyway. And he had little appreciation for W. H.'s fatigue and effort in the final game of his high school career. The Texas state championship meant nothing to Old Rip, nor did his grandson's all-consuming desire to get there.

On the night of that championship game, in early December, bits of skin, gristle, dried blood, and earth dangled in a gelatinous mass from W. H. Kelly's plastic face mask, swaying gently back and forth in rhythm with his gasping breath. He looked around him and checked the alignment of his teammates, bent on winning as he, and he crouched and waited. Sweat trickled from inside his football helmet, washed tiny creases in the dirt on his forehead, and burned into his blue eyes like slowly dripping acid. Fatigue threatened him. His body screamed for rest and struggled against the job before him for his attention. There was a deep, pulsing ache in his thigh, another at the point of his shoulder, and his face mask had again scooped skin and bone off the bridge of his nose.

That hadn't impressed Old Rip either. He, too, had known pain and a tired body that wanted to refuse the wishes of his mind.

Even when the Karankawa City home crowd came to its feet and began to chant, "War Hoss, War Hoss, War Hoss — *Wahhh Hoss*," Old Rip was still unimpressed. His grandson's name, William Henry Kelly, was good enough for Old Rip, and the town's nickname, "War Hoss," meant little to him.

The Karankawa Gators' slim, seven-six lead; the down and distance, fourth and two; the field position, W. H.'s feet planted on his own twenty-yard line as he aligned himself at middle linebacker;

nor the time left on the clock, fifty-seven seconds—none of it concerned Old Rip too much.

"It's just a damned *game*," he had often told W. H., and Old Rip hadn't understood when his grandson had tried to explain his feelings about football.

War Hoss Kelly delighted in the ability of his tall, thickly muscled frame to range from sideline to sideline making vicious tackles on running backs. Life was clean, simple, and violent on the football field, and he exulted in it. And sometimes, after a hard-fought game, he even found a perverse joy in sore muscles and deep bruises.

When W. H. felt the familiar, delicious shock travel from his thick neck to his churning legs as he drove his face mask into the fullback's chest and won the state championship for Karankawa City, Texas, Old Rip felt only one emotion. He was glad the season was finally over.

Now, as he pumped water, looked across the great stretch of Southeast Texas grass, and squinted against the July sun, the elder Kelly was worried. He was glad W. H.'s football was done and proud that his grandson had graduated, but he feared the ominous endings to come. The end of this ranch, coupled with W. H.'s going off to Texas State University on a football scholarship, were too horrible to contemplate. He hadn't been so sad and worried since his son had died when W. H. was nine.

And he was sorry he had been so hard on his son, Bill, about W. H.'s mother, Marcie.

Too often, Old Rip had thought back then, Bill let Marcie slip into tight blue jeans and go down to the VFW dances alone. Too often Bill was blind to the sultry glances Marcie flashed at the butcher in the Safeway store, the pharmacist at Walgreen's, or any cowboy on Main Street.

"You better treat her like a young horse," Old Rip had told his son. "You better keep her goddamn nose sore, or you gonna lose her. She'll buck you off and run away."

His words were prophetic. Marcie left a year before W. H.'s father beered up at the Black Cat Club, ran his pickup into a deep roadside ditch, and drowned.

The funeral was on a Saturday morning in the dead of winter, and Old Rip had squeezed a bawling W. H. in his lap as he suffered the consolation efforts of a Fundamentalist Church preacher. The following Monday W. H. was back in school and Old Rip was back at work in the oil refinery.

He worked in the refinery—"that damned coal-oil plant," he called it—solely to keep his ranch, cattle, and horses. He hated his refinery job, had always hated it, and even felt a rushing freedom surge deep inside him when he was fired from it.

"Laid off," his boss called it, "because them damned A-rabs and labor unions is killin' the company."

"I worked there all them years to preserve a way of life," he told his grandson, "to keep havin' this ranch and cattle. To keep cowboyin'. The damned *job* never meant nothin' to me."

His firing had come two years before W. H.'s graduation and seven years after the vice-president of the Great Coastal Bank had loaned him the money for more land and cattle.

"Practically shoveled it in my pocket," Old Rip told W. H.. "I had a good job at that damned coal-oil plant, a little land, and a few cattle—plenty collateral—and they was just dyin' to lend it. So like a damned fool, I took it. Me and everybody else thought prosperity was gonna last forever. Now they gonna take this place if I don't cough up the balloon payment by September."

"Well, shit, Rip," W. H. told his grandfather with the boundless enthusiasm of a nineteen-year-old, "I'll get me a summer job and we'll pay it."

That had been on the day after his graduation, two months before, and W. H. had managed to save a total of $726. The note at the Great Coastal Bank in Beaumont, Texas, was $5,000.

The round aluminum tank was rim full of water and overflowing before Old Rip quit pumping. He eyed it with satisfaction, took the straw hat off his graying mane of hair, and wiped sweat from his eyes with a dirty handkerchief. He whistled softly, "too-wheet," like a bobwhite quail, and looked around him.

The sorrel mare, Baby Doll, trotted up from behind him and drank from the clear water with long gulps. Old Rip watched the rippling movement of her throat as she swallowed, brushed black flies from her silky flank, and leaned against her with one arm thrown across her back.

43

She belonged to his grandson, and, not counting the Brahma, she was the most valuable animal on the place. W. H. had raised her from a colt, trained her, and there was no doubt that Baby Doll was one of the best quarter-mares in the county. The younger Kelly had refused two thousand dollars for her a year before, Old Rip remembered.

He looked toward the small copse of gnarled hackberry trees in the near pasture, saw cattle standing in the noon shade, and picked out the huge form of the Brahma. The bull was registered, gentle as only Brahma cattle can be, and had won blue ribbons at the county fair. The Brahma also belonged to W. H., was another result of his care and feeding, and was responsible for all the fat, white calves Old Rip loved to look at.

He walked away from the water tank and headed for the house, shaking his head. Two yellow cur-dogs—Mustard and Muriel—met him at the back porch, stretched their lanky frames lazily, and panted quietly with long, pink tongues dripping as he passed them and went into the house. The dogs were experts in cattle herding and/or cow catching, and they too were the personal property of W. H. Kelly.

Old Rip slammed the screen door behind him. "Goddammit, everything on the place—*wuth a shit*—belongs to the boy."

Mustard and Muriel lay quietly in the shade of a hackberry tree as Old Rip sliced neat, round holes in the sandy earth with the post-hole digger. Mending fences and digging post holes, jobs he put off till after five o'clock in summer, were occupying Old Rip's attention when W. H. got home from his job with the county. He knew W. H. was almost home before he heard, or saw, the decrepit old Ford pickup they shared; the dogs began barking their happy bark and raced off toward the house while the truck was a half-mile down the highway. It was a daily ritual with them, and Old Rip never ceased to be amazed at their sharp hearing. There were probably scores of identical old trucks that passed the ranch each day, but Mustard and Muriel somehow knew the sound of W. H.'s truck. And Old Rip wished he knew how they could discern the difference.

He stopped work and leaned on the post-hole digger, watching W. H. step down from the truck, kneel, and embrace both the dogs, which were jumping and cavorting as if they hadn't seen the boy for months. They licked the face of Old Rip's grandson and acted like puppies. "I *know* he's seen them two dogs eat horse-turds," Old Rip said to himself, "and how he can let 'em lick him in the face is beyond me."

W. H. Kelly ran into the house and Old Rip continued his work on the fence. Five minutes later the boy trotted up to his grandfather with a half-eaten sandwich in his hand. "Hey, Rip," W. H. said, "how's it goin'?"

"Dammit, boy," the old man growled, "I hope you washed your hands after you played with them two shit-eatin' old dogs. But I'll bet a purty you didn't."

W. H. Kelly stood six feet, two inches and shirtless as he ate the rest of his sandwich with unwashed hands, and his heavily muscled chest and shoulders gleamed with a light sweat. He regarded Old Rip with suspicious eyes. "Okay, Rip, what's wrong?"

"I'm wonderin' why the hell I'm botherin' with this old fence, that's what's wrong. I'm wonderin' why I don't just let the gaddamned Great Coastal Bank fix their own fences."

W. H. nodded, looked at the ground, and, with a booted foot, began rearranging a pile of dirt Old Rip had made with the post-hole digger. "I figured that was it. Hell, Rip, we ain't gonna lose this ranch, we'll figure somethin'; we always have."

Old Rip shook his head, "You've got that a little wrong, son. Fact is, *I've* always figured somethin'. You've mostly played football."

W. H. Kelly's blue eyes flashed fire at his grandfather for a moment, then softened and he spoke quietly. "That ain't quite fair, Rip, and you know it. I've worked my ass off on this place . . . you just tell me what you want me to do, and I'll damned sure do it."

"You're right, son. Well, maybe half right, anyway. You have worked hard, but you've done precious little thinkin', and I figure it's time you started to *think.*"

They worked till dark repairing the fence, and the only words spoken were those necessary to finish the job. They had fought before, had arguments, and on a few occasions had almost come to blows, but W. H. sensed that this was different. And he went to bed bewildered and not understanding what his grandfather wanted him to do. He slept little that night. The next day his co-workers on the county road saw a difference in him and, after a few attempts at humor, they let him alone.

It took two days for him to figure it out, and when he did, he didn't like it much. But there didn't appear to be any other way, and he broached the subject to Old Rip on Saturday, during his weekend break from the county job. "What do you reckon the Brahma's worth?"

"Not near enough," his grandfather answered in his direct way, knowing immediately what W. H. was driving at. "But I'm proud you come to it by your-own-self."

"You mean I've got to sell Baby Doll too?"

They were in the process of nailing corrugated tin on the roof of the barn, and Old Rip looked his grandson full in the face, sat down on the hot roof and sighed. He nodded slowly. "I 'spect so. And maybe the dogs, too."

W. H. Kelly ran a hand through his red hair and narrowed his eyes, "Goddammit, Rip, you're talkin' about everything I own in this world."

"I know it, son, and I'm sorry as hell about that. But look at it another way . . . where the hell you gonna keep them animals if we lose this place? In that damned dormitory up at the university?"

"Can't we sell some calves if the Brahma ain't enough?"

Old Rip nodded, "Sure, we can sell calves, but what the hell we gonna live on afterwards?"

"Shit-fahr!" Old Rip growled as they pulled the stock trailer loaded with all W. H.'s animals toward downtown Beaumont, Texas. "I've got to deposit my whole Social *In*security check to make up the dif-ference. Lester Prince is a thief."

Old Rip loved to talk about the "Social *In*security" the federal government offered. He often instructed W. H. to study carefully the utterings of politicians and great conglomerates, then think about the direct opposite of whatever they said. And today, as they headed to the Great Coastal Bank to deposit his check before hauling W. H.'s possessions to Lester Prince's ranch, he was especially vocal.

"The opposite is a hell-of-a-lot closer to the truth," he reminded his grandson once more. "You hear all them fellers sayin' they in 'oil production'? Hell, they don't produce oil, they destroy it—they

46

really in oil *destruction*, son. They hate the truth worse than the devil hates holy water . . . and don't never believe they give a rat's ass about you. Try to imagine yourself as a tool—try to be a damned *shovel* for a minute—then you'll get some idea how they see you."

Had it been possible to sell the animals separately, Old Rip thought, maybe to some dude townfolks who might regard them as pets, they might have brought more money. Maybe the Brahma, halter-broken to lead and willing to let himself be rubbed and petted, would have made a great backyard conversation piece for some affluent doctor or engineer bent on impressing his peers. But such was not to be. The Brahma, Baby Doll, and the dogs had to be sold to a hard-headed, conservative rancher who had very practical ideas for their future use. And that man, Lester Prince, like hundreds of other Texas ranchers, including Rip Kelly, was determined to buy as cheaply as he could.

After casting about for two weeks, Lester Prince was the only prospective buyer Old Rip could find, and his final offer for all the animals was $4,800. "Prince ain't no better than the damned bank," the old man continued his tirade against the society he blamed for his grandson's loss, "and the damned bank ain't no better than the politicians. When a poor man has to depend on the goodness of unregulated corporations for the necessities of life, he's in deep trouble."

He held the old truck in the road with one hand, used the other to accentuate his points, and cast sidelong glances at W. H. to see his reaction. W. H. stared straight ahead at the highway, flint-visaged and quiet in his anger and sadness, and he wished his grandfather would just shut up for a while.

"As far as I can see, Rip," W. H. said, "it don't make a hell of a lot of difference whose fault it is. My animals are good as gone. I wish you'd just leave it alone."

Old Rip sighed and nodded. "Well, hand me that bottle again, I'm dry as a old snakeskin." He indicated the glove compartment where he kept the bottle of Old Crow.

"You been hittin' that pretty steady," W. H. Kelly told Old Rip as he handed him the bottle, "and you're drivin'."

"Horseshit," Rip Kelly growled as he pulled from the bottle.

The goosenecked stock trailer the Kellys pulled behind them had

seen better days. Its hardwood floor was worn down to about half
its original thickness; many points where its steel frame had been
welded together were badly rusted; its gates—both the middle one
that separated the Brahma from the horse and the tailgate that let
the stock enter the trailer—were bent from years of hard use, and
their latches were suspect. The trailer rattled loudly, and each time
the bull or horse shifted its weight, the whole rig swayed erratically.
Old Rip had to fight the pickup to keep it on the road. Mustard
and Muriel stood in a corner at the rear of the trailer with Baby
Doll and watched her movements closely. Every time the mare moved,
the dogs were in danger of being stepped on by a thousand-pound
horse. The trailer had no top, no covering against the blazing Texas
sun, and the animals suffered.

The trailer and truck advertised the Kellys' poverty and, to the
practiced eyes of any amateur social scientist, their redneckery and
country pride as well. Such sights were seldom seen in downtown
Beaumont, Texas—a city that viewed itself as an up-and-coming
younger version of Houston, despite its urban decay, social problems, and a misplaced and overweening arrogance. Those men and
women who walked briskly down its sidewalks, clad in dacron and
polyester suits of various gray shades and carrying briefcases, frowned
and eyed the Kelly entourage and barking dogs with disdain.

W. H. was unaware of their frowns and disfavor, but Old Rip
both saw and felt their stares, "Look at 'em," he said, waving his
arm to indicate all of Beaumont, Texas. "Don't know whether a horse
sleeps on the ground or roosts in a tree."

In mere miles, Rip Kelly reckoned his ranch was separated from
Beaumont by forty; but in attitude and values by light-years. It was
another facet of his intuition and sensitivity that Old Rip could
never satisfactorily explain to his grandson. And, in traversing that
forty miles, the old man had partaken of a goodly portion of the
Old Crow. Which was why he paid more attention to the business
types on the sidewalks of Beaumont than to his driving.

It was also the reason he ran through the stoplight a half-block
from the Great Coastal Bank, hit the city bus squarely amidships,
and obliterated the sign on the side of the bus that said: EAT MORE
BEEF.

The sound of the crash echoed up and down the walled street

48

of Beaumont, Texas, like an explosion. Occupants of the bus were thrown from their seats into the aisle. The bus driver, who had had no warning and hadn't seen what had hit him, applied the brakes too late to avoid knocking over a light pole, but in time to keep from running the bus into a plate glass window. The gray-suited and serious professionals on the sidewalk, many of whom were headed for the Great Coastal Bank, lost their somberness. Women screamed and men stopped dead in their tracks as their mouths formed imperfect O's.

Old Rip was momentarily stunned and W. H. Kelly, who had watched fascinated and speechless as EAT MORE BEEF grew ever larger in his vision before the impact, was out of the pickup door before the dust settled.

The animals didn't fare as well.

The rusty trailer jackknifed to a sixty-degree angle and both Baby Doll and the Brahma fell to the floor. The shock jarred the middle gate latch loose and the Brahma, trying to struggle to his feet, bumped it and it swung open. The huge bull, gentle or not, was terribly frightened and lunged against the steel prong of the gate latch; it jabbed into his right eye and neatly scooped out his eyeball. Baby Doll—fully saddled and bridled—was fighting to regain her feet, and just as she succeeded, the Brahma hit her in the side with his massive head. He knocked her against the railed side of the trailer, but she recovered quickly, wheeled about, and began kicking at him.

Mustard and Muriel, true to cur-dog nature, jumped nimbly about trying to avoid the hooves of horse and bull, and went into a veritable paroxysm of barking.

Steam and smoke rose from the engine of the Ford pickup and its horn screamed an unceasing wail into the street. The bull snorted and roared, the dogs bayed and growled as if they were in mortal conflict, and some fifteen frightened passengers streamed out of the city bus.

Such was the sensory overload that greeted W. H. Kelly as he arrived at the rear of the trailer. He immediately saw the impossibility of separating the horse and bull into their respective fore and aft compartments, so, fearing for their safety, he did the next best thing. He opened the rear gate, waded into the melee, and was promptly knocked flat by the bellowing and bleeding bull. The Brahma ran on past him and leaped to the pavement of downtown Beaumont. Baby Doll started out too, but stepped on a bridle rein when she reached the street and came to a halt. Mustard and Muriel flashed by a prone W. H. Kelly and ran straight toward the retreating bull.

To understand what happened next, one must know something about Texas cur-dogs. First, they are born with a desire to catch cattle, hogs, or goats. No one knows why; perhaps it's a throwback to ancient wolf ancestors, or maybe it's the result of generations of doing this work. Second, they are trained to catch ornery and re-calcitrant animals that refuse to be herded—herd-quitters, as it were. As long as cattle stay docile and together, moving along in quiet obedience as their masters require, the dogs merely bark. But if an errant animal quits the herd, runs away on its own, they become vicious catchers instead of herders.

Mustard and Muriel regarded the Brahma's abrupt departure as herd-quitting, and they raced to turn him back and teach him some discipline. Mustard ran past him on his left, the side where he still had eyesight, and he lowered his head to fight the dog. But he couldn't see Muriel, and as he stopped and turned to do battle with her mate, she latched on to his right ear with sharp, powerful teeth. He turned his full attention to her—and Mustard darted in and got a firm bite on the area between his nostrils, and hung on. The Brahma raised his great head then, attempting to fling the dog away from him, but Mustard held on with the ferocity of centuries, and the bull turned a half-circle before the cur released his grip. The dogs had turned him around, and now they headed him back toward the trailer wreck, W. H. Kelly, and the milling people, at a dead run.

W. H. had temporarily lost his ability to breathe when the Brahma had knocked him to the dung-splattered floor of the trailer. He had lain there, struggling to regain his breath, for what seemed long min-utes. By the time the dogs turned the bull, W. H. was sitting on the edge of the trailer. Old Rip was standing—unhurt, but befuddled, shocked, and drunk—beside the wreckage, ignoring the screamed curses of the bus driver, as spectators and bus passengers began to edge toward W. H. in wary solicitude for his health.

W. H. figured most of them had never seen anyone get run over by a Brahma bull.

The Great Coastal Bank loomed darkly a half-block away. An

architectural plagiarism of the staid and stodgy moneylending tem-
ples of Houston and Dallas, and a memorial to collective lack of
imagination of its board of directors, it reflected the city's dedica-
tion to the new, the flashy, and the temporary. Before its electronic
doors, small groups of people gathered and pointed toward the Kellys'
wreck. And inside the bank, tellers flashed plastic smiles as fully
automatic as the bank's doors, and told their customers, "Have a
nice day."

W. H. Kelly got to his feet, tightened the cinch on a trembling
Baby Doll, and climbed aboard her as the dogs chased the bull
down the sidewalk, past the wreckage and toward the Great Coastal
Bank. Solicitous spectators scattered in all directions and the sidewalk was instantly cleared for the bull's passage.

"Where the hell you goin', boy?" Old Rip had come to his senses
and stood watching W. H. on shaky legs.

W. H. applied his booted heels to Baby Doll and was taking his
lariat rope from the saddlehorn. The little mare bolted past Old Rip
in a blur of motion and W. H. whispered through clenched teeth,
"To catch my damned bull, Rip." And War Hoss Kelly's eyes filmed
over, grew glassy with the same madness they had in the midst of
a football game. He looked forward to the release that action would
bring.

Mustard and Muriel had worked their way past the bull and
stopped him again. He lowered his head, bellowed, and tried to gore
them with huge horns. W. H. got close enough to cast his rope just
as Mustard once more got a death grip on the bull's nose. W. H.
made his throw but the noose was deflected by a street sign. He
missed.

Baby Doll, as she was trained to do, came to a sudden stop when
W. H. threw the rope. She almost set her rump down on the sidewalk and sparks flew from her steel-shod hooves.

"Turn him loose, Mustard," W. H. screamed as he began re-coiling
his rope for another throw. It was hard to rope the bull's horns
while he was constantly moving his head to fight the dogs off.

Mustard did as he was told, but as soon as he released his grip,
the Brahma ran—straight for the electronic doors of the Great Coastal
Bank.

Once more War Hoss Kelly dug his heels into Baby Doll's ribs, but he was too late; the bull was within thirty feet of the bank's main entrance. W. H. then countermanded his previous order to the cur-dogs, "Catch him! Goddammit, catch him!"

They caught him at the precise moment when he reached the electronic eye in front of the bank. The doors opened and the Brahma burst into the posh lobby of the Great Coastal Bank with a large, yellow cur-dog hanging from each ear, blood running down his head, and a roar in his throat.

In the swiftness of his passing, War Hoss Kelly had not seen Channel 88 Television's mobile unit parked in front of the bank. All his concentrated energy centered on the Brahma, Mustard and Muriel, and his effort to manage the excited thousand-pound mare. He was busy calculating time, distance, and pursuit angles, and his mind refused to comprehend extraneous details. Thus he had no way of knowing that, inside the lobby, Channel 88 was in the process of filming a corporate profile on the Great Coastal Bank.

The bank floor was smooth and slick with layers of wax and polish, and the Brahma was the victim of both his blind eye and the bank president's penchant for shine. The bull blundered into a customer service table as he swung his head back and forth, trying to dislodge determined dogs. He knocked the table over, sent blank deposit slips and bank propaganda pamphlets flying, scattered customers, lost his footing, and fell sprawling on the bank floor. Mustard and Muriel quickly released their ear-holds and began to chew at whatever portions of the Brahma they could reach. He was down at their eye level now, and as they chewed on targets of opportunity, he bellowed and tried mightily to regain his feet. Blood ran freely from his eye socket onto the bank floor, his hard hooves had trouble finding purchase on the waxed surface, and as he struggled, the unnerved Brahma began to defecate in a loose, brown-green stream. As the bull succeeded in standing up, War Hoss Kelly entered the bank astride a running horse, swinging a lariat rope and screaming at the dogs, "Turn him loose!"

A fat lady in pink hair curlers at a teller's window fainted dead away. Two men in three-piece, Brooks Brothers suits fought to get behind the counter, and the bank guard—recently retired from the police force and disappointed because he never had enough opportunities to use the pistol at his hip—drew the gun from its holster and tried to decide what to shoot first. The photographer from the Channel 88 Big Eye kept his wits about him, climbed atop the tellers' counter and solemnly taped the action.

Mustard and Muriel, ever obedient to their master, turned and trotted away from the stricken bull, dripped saliva on the bank floor, flopped down with tongues drooling beside the tellers' counter, and looked at W. H. for further instructions. Baby Doll had the same problem with the waxed and polished floor as the Brahma: she slipped and stumbled to her knees and W. H. was hard put to keep his seat. He watched helplessly as the bull disappeared through the electronic doors at the other end of the long bank lobby.

W. H. sighed, dismounted, and began to tighten the saddle girt. It was in his mind that roping the Brahma would certainly require all his rigging to be intact and tight, and he was as oblivious to the shouts and moans from those inside the bank as he would have been to screaming football fans. He simply didn't hear them; nor was he aware of the white-faced, tight-lipped bank guard until that uniformed officer grabbed him by the shoulder, put the pistol in his back, and roughly jerked him around.

Cur-dogs are also possessive and protective of what they regard as their own. Mustard and Muriel were especially so, and when they saw the man put his hands on W. H., they reacted without the slightest hesitation. Muriel leaped and grabbed a great chunk of the officer's soft buttocks while Mustard sprang at his throat, knocking him down on the shit-slick bank floor. The jar of his overweight body hitting the floor knocked the pistol loose from his fingers and the gun slid to rest against the overturned customer service table.

"Turn him loose!" W. H. yelled at the dogs before they could maul the man further.

The bank guard lay moaning on the floor, and W. H. got back on the mare and calmly began coiling his rope as Baby Doll, too, relieved herself in the lobby of the Great Coastal Bank. He whistled at the dogs and started the mare toward the far end of the lobby where the Brahma had exited.

Mustard and Muriel followed, but the male dog stopped and sniffed at an overturned table, raised his leg, and let forth a golden stream on it before W. H. Kelly and his animals finally left the bank.

The younger Kelly hadn't been gone for more than two minutes when Old Rip entered the bank building, carrying under his arm what was left of the fifth of Old Crow. He looked around at the overturned tables, the blood and dung, the dazed and disheveled people, and mumbled to himself, "Yep. I believe they come through here alright," then ambled up to a teller's window.

He leaned against the counter and watched as a janitor shuffled toward the smeared floor with a mop and push broom. He didn't understand why the young man from Channel 88 wouldn't let the janitor clean up the mess. "Don't you dare *touch* that," the young man ordered the bank custodian as he beckoned the photographer. And Old Rip was further confused when the cameraman kneeled and minutely examined and filmed a neat pile of horse apples in the lobby of one of the largest banks in the great Southwest.

"Can't a man get no service here?" Old Rip pounded on the counter and looked for a teller.

A young woman with her hairdo askew hurried toward him from the center of the lobby where she had watched, fascinated, as the Channel 88 camerman filmed the pile of horse droppings. Hoping she would be on TV for the six o'clock news, she had stood as close to the dung and blood as possible, trying to smooth a hairdo that fitted her head like a gold-painted football helmet. She wore slacks—a new dispensation of the Great Coastal Bank that was supposed to prove its basic tolerance and down-to-earth attitude.

"I'm sorry," she told the old man, "but you wouldn't believe what just happened here. We just had a bull, a man on a horse, and two dogs run through the lobby."

Rip Kelly eyed the rubble and excrement around him. "Naw. You gotta be shittin' me!"

He endorsed the check, gave the excited young woman instructions to apply it to the balloon note, walked to the Trailways bus station, and bought a ticket back to Karankawa City, Texas. He left the old truck and trailer for the law to dispose of, and as he took his seat on the bus he told himself, "Hell, that boy'll be alright. He

54

knows big weeds from bushes." Then he took a long swallow from the whiskey bottle and settled down for the trip home.

The Brahma *was* gentle, despite Lester Prince's ravings to the contrary after he saw the bull raging through the bank lobby with an eyeball gone and blood streaming down his head on the Channel 88 ten o'clock news. Lester called Old Rip that night to tell him the deal was off. "I ain't buyin' no damned one-eyed bull that's crazy enough to run through a bank scarin' the hell out of people," he yelled at Old Rip.

"Fuck you, Lester," Rip Kelly answered, "I didn't want to sell him to you anyhow. And the bull *is* gentle. I never allowed he was *saddle-broke*—or house-broke like a six-week-old puppy." And Old Rip slammed the receiver back on its hook with a force that proved the solidity of AT&T products.

As he trotted through the streets of Beaumont, the bull was seen by scores of people. But W. H., only a few minutes behind him, was unable to catch him. And he suddenly disappeared from sight around two in the afternoon, somewhere in the quiet and exclusive tree-shaded neighborhoods of West Beaumont. W. H. rode the little mare through the fashionable area in vain, and Mustard and Muriel were of less help than usual because, W. H. believed, the smells of the city overwhelmed them with carbon monoxide and conflicting odors. Channel 88's mobile unit followed wherever he went, as did a black and white patrol car of the Beaumont Police. It was after two-thirty when he decided to rest, and he rode Baby Doll into a shaded spot on a vacant lot and unsaddled her. The police car and Channel 88's Big Eye van parked nearby and their occupants got out and joined him.

The policemen were courteous and considerate. They even explained how they commiserated with him, and as he answered their questions about the wreck and what happened afterward, the Channel 88 camera dutifully taped everything. It wasn't until the police finished and walked back to their vehicle that the Channel 88 reporter made the proposition to W. H. Kelly.

"If you can keep this chase going for a while," the reporter said, "I can almost *guarantee* you national coverage. This is one of the best human interest stories I've ever seen, but it would be more exciting if it lasted longer."

W. H. Kelly stared at the man, shook his head without answering, and stretched out in the shade to rest and think. The camera traced his every movement.

The Brahma wasn't hiding; he was tired. He found a two-acre lawn surrounding the mansion of one of the Beaumont rich, walked in under the shade of its tall pine trees behind a neatly trimmed, four-foot hedge, and lay down to rest. He woke up about four o'clock, considerably quietened, and began eating the monkey grass along the edges of the curving driveway. It was the yelling of the mansion yard man, newly arrived from Piedras Negras, that alerted W. H. to the bull's whereabouts. He was less than a half-block away and W. H.'s high school Spanish was enough to tell him what the screams meant. "Ayiie, un toro mas grande!" the man screamed as he ran down the quiet street toward W. H., the police car, and Channel 88's mobile unit.

It took only minutes for W. H. to saddle the mare and ride to the pleasing expanse of cultivated St. Augustine grass where the bull grazed. Channel 88 and the police followed, but the news reporter was disappointed. W. H. saw the Brahma, got off his horse with the lariat rope in his hand, and walked slowly toward the bull. He spoke softly, "Easy now, Brahma, easy now." And the gigantic animal stood and looked at W. H. Kelly with his one good eye until the boy stood beside him. He stood quietly as W. H. fashioned a halter around his horns and head with the rope. Then W. H. led the bull back to his horse, mounted, and told the incredulous spectators, "He's really a gentle bull, he was just hurt and scared, that's all."

W. H. had been far too busy to consider what he was going to do once he caught the bull. As he led the Brahma through late afternoon traffic on a tired and hungry Baby Doll, trying to watch bull, dogs, and drivers unaccustomed to seeing large animals on the highway, he instinctively headed for Interstate 10. That was the way home, and he didn't know what else to do since the truck and trailer were wrecked and he had no idea where his grandfather was. Channel 88 dogged his heels until five o'clock.

Sometime after nine, after the sun had disappeared into the western horizon and he was plodding down the freeway in gathering darkness, he was besieged by trucks pulling stock trailers. Three of them arrived almost simultaneously and their drivers practically begged him to load his animals and let them drive him home. He accepted the first offer, and it was easy work to load the Brahma, who had been loaded and unloaded many times. Baby Doll and the dogs were absolutely eager to get inside the open trailer and rest.

"My name's John Cleary," the samaritan told W. H., "and me and the wife saw you on the teevee at six-thirty. I told her, 'Shirley,' I said, 'That boy's gonna need some help.' Where's your granddaddy, War Hoss?" The man was tall, about forty years old, and obviously knowledgeable about W. H.'s problems.

W. H. looked at the man and asked, "How did you know about my grandfather?"

"Hell, he was on the teevee too. Channel 88 went plumb down to your place to interview him . . . don't want to make you mad, but does he drink a lot? He sure gave them teevee people some kinda hell about mindin' their own business and stayin' outa his."

"Yeah," W. H. nodded, "sometimes he drinks."

They unloaded the animals beside the barn. W. H. put the Brahma in a small pen where he would be available for shots of penicillin and Terramycin the next morning. Old Rip was not around and still had not appeared when W. H. thanked John Cleary and the man drove off through the gate in front of the ranch house.

It was ten-thirty by then, and he found the old man sitting in the kitchen, staring at the wall and mumbling to himself. "It's all over. Truck's gone, trailer's gone, and they gonna take this ranch next."

W. H. sat down across the table from his grandfather. "Hell, Rip, don't take it so hard. We still got the animals sold, we'll get 'em to Lester Prince some damned way."

Old Rip shood his head sadly. "Nope. I just talked to him, he backed out. It's all over."

A week passed, and neither W. H. nor his grandfather could find a solution to the problem. The realization was slow in coming, but when it finally did, W. H. mentally kissed his football scholarship to Texas State University goodbye. He could not even think about joining the Lobos and leaving Old Rip alone at a time like this. Where would the old man go? W. H. asked himself. What would he do? How would he survive alone in the world without any family except his grandson? He called the university and told the coach he would not be reporting for football practice or school, and he explained why.

"I wish I could help you, son," the TSU coach said sadly, "but there just ain't no way. The NCAA is heavy on our tail right now, and till you've had them on your tail, you don't know what trouble can be."

Another week passed before the small, quiet man dressed in faded Levis drove up into the yard wanting to buy a Brahma bull. He lived in Conroe, Texas, he explained, and he had seen the bull on television a couple of weeks before when he was in Beaumont. "The Brahma looked pretty good to me," the man told Old Rip and W. H. in a soft voice, "even with one eyeball."

"Well he's damned sure for sale," Old Rip said, "but I 'spect we'll have to get a powerful bunch of money for him. Hell, I reckon that damned bull's worth five thousand dollars, and that's what it'll take to buy him."

The man sat down on the tailgate of the new pickup he had driven up in and grinned at Old Rip. "We got kind of a ticklish situation here, Mr. Kelly. See I *know* what's at stake here. I know you need that much to ease by the bank note. And I don't believe you can make it long on just five thousand, not with your pickup wrecked and your trailer gone . . . and you facing a Driving While Intoxicated charge that might put you in jail. Naw, there ain't no way I can give you that much money for the bull."

"What the hell you drivin' at, mister?" W. H. had stood and listened quietly to the exchange between the stranger and his grandfather. "You figure to *steal* the damned bull from us because we're in such terrible shape?"

The man put up his hands in protest and shook his head. "Now you wait just a minute, War Hoss, and hear me out before you go to flyin' off the handle. Why don't ya'll just *lease* me the bull? Why don't we just leave him here and let me send down, oh say four or five good cows, and pay ya'll for his services, and your care for my cattle? Say I pay Mr. Kelly six hundred a month for those services

. . . in addition to some up-front money, say that five thousand ya'll owe the bank? How will that be?"

The Kellys stood and stared at each other for a full minute before either of them answered the soft-spoken little man. It was just too much, too good to be true, and their disbelief quickly turned to suspicion. "What the hell's your angle, mister?" Old Rip asked. "You pissin' on my leg, or what?"

"No sir," the man said softly, "I'm just offerin' you the best deal I can. I ain't got no angle, Mr. Kelly."

"*You got to have a angle.* There ain't nobody fool enough to come all the way—clean from Conroe—just to give us money. And a perfect stranger at that."

The little man in Levis smiled broadly, "I guess you got me, Mr. Kelly. I'll come clean. Let's just say I'm a football fan that hates to see a bright youngster, like War Hoss here, lose the chance for a good education."

"Well, bullshit . . ." Old Rip began, but a light went on in W. H.'s mind and he stopped his grandfather.

"Don't look a gift horse in the goddamned mouth, Rip. Let it alone, I'll explain later. Mister, the bull belongs to me, and I accept your offer."

The stranger wrote them a check for five thousand dollars, explained how he would send the monthly checks and ship the cattle for the bull to service, then he left. And as he drove down the driveway of the Kelly Ranch, Old Rip stood and watched with eyes still narrowed with suspicion. "He'll find some way to get to us, boy. I ain't never seen it fail."

W. H. Kelly grinned at his grandfather for a long minute and began to laugh. He looked at the check in his hand, looked at Old Rip, and laughed some more. He held his sides and laughed until Mustard and Muriel joined in and began barking and romping around him like little children enjoying the best fun they had had since school was out for the summer. He bent over laughing, and when he glanced up and saw the solemn and serious expression on Rip's face, he laughed until tears came to his eyes.

"Goddam, Rip . . ." he choked out between peals of laughter that had become sobs. "Goddam, the man's a TSU *Lobo!* He's one of them folks everybody makes jokes about. He's one o' them 'football nuts' you spent my whole high school career cussin'. He represents what you've always told me was 'damned foolishness and a waste of time,' and he just saved your cussed old crotchety *ass*!"

When autumn came to Southeast Texas that year, after W. H. moved into the dormitory, Old Rip pumped water from the old pitcher-pump and watched white geese fly in from Canada. They came with frosty wings, powerful and swooping in like ghostly wraiths from a time-dimmed past only they remembered. Their raucous voices cracked the cooling air with the telling of a winter place— this flat coastal land stretching from the Gulf of Mexico to the Texas horizon—and Rip Kelly was sure they spoke a genetic memory; passing on an unbroken story of life. And when he looked southward to the Gulf, his mind could see teeming millions of organisms the marsh maintained, and his eyes could see it covered with such an expanse of blue sky dotted with clouds that he was awestruck, like a child, with wonder. At the precise point where the marsh grew in wild, green profusion from the shells-ground-to-sand of ancient crustaceans and almost touched the sea that baked and boiled it all together like a gigantic bouillabaisse, he could imagine a genesis . . . He was certain he was witnessing miracles.

Two years later, in his sophomore year at Texas State University, as War Hoss Kelly lined up at middle linebacker against Texas A&M before a screaming crowd of eighty thousand people, at Kyle Field in College Station, Old Rip stood and screamed like a drill instructor, "Bust-em, Lobos! Goddamn, *bust-em*!"

Joe Willie's Problem

Joe Willie Kolander was a descendant of one of the families who founded Karankawa County, it is said. But many Karankawans aren't sure he even exists, and few are willing to discuss him at all. The ones who will talk about about him, like Sheriff Little Boy Jefferson, say he was forced to live in a different world; the world of his mind, for the most part, in a cabin on the edge of Brand's Bayou some seven miles removed from the nearest human habitation. He had a real problem and his ultraconservative family wanted to keep it confined to Karankawa County. They succeeded for almost fifty years.

Joe Willie's problem manifested itself in 1934, a few weeks after he was born. His mother told him she first began to notice it when his baby buggy wouldn't work correctly. She was proud of Joe Willie, as only a young mother with her firstborn can be, and the very first time she put him in the buggy and started down the quiet, tree-shaded street in Karankawa City, one wheel came off and dumped him onto the sidewalk. She picked him up tenderly and clucked in his ear as she carried him home, pulling the broken buggy behind her.

Joe Willie's father, besides being a rich Dutchman, was a master mechanic who took much pleasure in his ability to fix things. He re-attached the wheel and told his wife, "There now! I'll guarantee you this wheel won't come off anymore!" And Mr. Kolander went away to oversee his vast holdings of marsh grass, range cattle, and oil wells in perfect confidence, for he could fix every conceivable kind of machine.

And although Joe Willie's mother knew her husband was a great mechanic, she wasn't taking any chances with the safety of her baby son. She tested the buggy with the thoroughness of a good Dutch wife before she put Joe Willie in it. She loaded it down with heavy books of a weight some five times Joe Willie's, and she pushed it all around the house to make sure. The buggy worked fine.

Then, when she put Joe Willie in it and started down the same sidewalk, a wheel collapsed and folded down on itself as if overloaded. And from that day on, Mrs. Kolander carried Joe Willie. She never trusted baby buggies again.

At the same time Joe Willie's baby bed, from which he cooed and gah-gahed, had problems too. It had castors on it, and they worked fine as long as they only had to bear his weight. But every time Mrs. Kolander tried to roll Joe Willie in the bed so that she could sweep under it, or give him a change of scenery, a castor came off. And it was never the same wheel; they seemed to alternate.

Soon Joe Willie's parents came to notice how their car, a new Chevrolet, would work wonderfully until they put him inside it. Sometimes it wouldn't even start when he was in it. Other times it might quit miles away from their home, stranding them in strange places with a small baby.

When he was six years old, Joe Willie was really looking forward to beginning school. He stood neat and starched in his overalls with the crossed galluses in the back, his face scrubbed and shining, his hair slicked back, his tablet, crayons, and a red Coca-Cola pencil clutched tightly in his little fist, smiling at the world while he waited for the school bus that first day. But the bus belched a great puff of black smoke as it pulled up even with him and stopped. It wheezed, coughed, and died before he could get inside it, and the black smoke and flying dust it generated covered Joe Willie, and when it cleared he stood there covered with black soot, crying.

They never could get the bus started that morning, and they hauled it off with a wrecker after Joe Willie was gone. The school sent another bus and transferred him and the other kids onto it, and it broke down a block from school. All the children had to walk the rest of the way. That morning was only the beginning of Joe Willie's problems at school.

Mrs. Lucas, Joe Willie's first-grade teacher, was conscientious about teaching and keeping her room orderly—she was a Dutch descendant too and had an atavistic Teutonic tendency to tidiness that turned to tyranny on occasion. She showed all her pupils how the pencil sharpener worked and lined them up to try it; Mrs. Lucas didn't want any dawdling at the pencil sharpener to interrupt her carefully scheduled day. Joe Willie was third in line, and when his turn came he inserted his red Coca-Cola pencil, turned the handle, and watched as it came off in his hand. He thought it was just like tearing a drumstick off a roast duck.

Mrs. Lucas was annoyed, but she was nice enough about it. All the other children, of course, laughed at Joe Willie and he felt terrible about the pencil sharpener. But the teacher gave him a tight-lipped smile and told him, "Don't worry, we'll get another one."

She did. And when the janitor had it installed and Joe Willie's turn came again it just froze up on him . . . locked. After Joe Willie's teacher ordered her *third* pencil sharpener on the first day of school, the principal brought it down himself. He was a jolly fellow, all smiles, and he looked on it as a great joke on Mrs. Lucas when she explained what had happened. He stood there chuckling after the new sharpener was screwed into the wall by the blackboard. "Step up there and sharpen your pencil, young man," he nodded at Joe Willie.

Joe Willie did, and the handle turned alright. It didn't come off in his hand, but it made a terrible racket and the boy thought it was awfully hard to turn. "Hold up, Joe Willie," the principal said.

He took the housing off the pencil sharpener. "I'll swear, Mrs. Lucas," the principal stood there and shook his head. "All the teeth on this thing are completely stripped. Maybe we got a bad batch of these." Then he turned and looked at Joe Willie with a strange expression, and he seemed to have lost his sense of humor.

But Mrs. Lucas never let Joe Willie sharpen another pencil, not that day or any other day; she simply didn't have time to waste on pencil sharpeners. So when his pencil got dull, someone else had to sharpen it for him and he was embarrassed and his feelings were hurt. When school was out that day, Joe Willie unknowingly did a bad thing. He saw Mrs. Lucas's car parked in the parking lot and, childlike, played at having a pistol in his hand. He pointed a forefinger at the car and said, "Pow!"

The left front tire of Mrs. Lucas's car went flat.

His condition worsened. When he went to junior high—by then all the teachers had learned not to let him sharpen a pencil—there were ceiling fans in all the classrooms. And, like most other kids, whenever Joe Willie was taking a test he stared up at the ceiling to concentrate. He had to be very careful about that, since if he stared too long at one of those fans a blade would fall off. Which was dangerous to other people, Joe Willie knew, but sometimes forgot; and his teachers learned simply to yell at him when they saw him doing it. "Don't look at that fan, Joe Willie! Look out the window or somewhere!" For teachers can accustom themselves to almost anything after understanding—and for decades, living with—the idiosyncrasies of children, parents, and school administrators.

But Joe Willie learned that looking outside could be dangerous too. One day in late spring, right after a teacher yelled at him for looking at a fan, Joe Willie looked out the window just as poor old Mr. Young was passing on his tractor. He was mowing the campus grass, and Joe Willie was concentrating on the geography test so hard that he didn't realize he was staring, and Mr. Young's tractor overheated. The cap blew off the radiator, and hot water and steam scalded Mr. Young. Joe Willie hated that because he really liked Mr. Young.

Then came high school. And some idiot of an assistant principal, newly hired in Karankawa City and trying to impress, put Joe Willie Kolander in a typing class. Joe Willie went to the new principal and tried to explain how it was impossible for him to get along with machines, told him how it could be dangerous to the teacher and the other kids. But the principal thought Joe Willie was trying to get out of a distasteful class, and said as much.

It was one of the rare occasions Joe Willie ever got mad. He went to the typing room and stomped in. Mrs. Allen, the typing teacher, knew about Joe Willie's affliction. "My God," Mrs. Allen yelled, "Joe Willie Kolander, you get out of here right now. We got several thousands of dollars worth of 'quipment in here."

Joe Willie heard her, but he was mad at the new principal so he didn't move for a minute. He hesitated, and while he was standing there he zeroed in on Mrs. Allen's typewriter. "Blip-blam!" Joe Willie said to the typewriter, and it began making noises like old pieces of iron being shaken in an aluminum bucket.

"Get the hell out of here, Joe Willie!" Mrs. Allen screamed, forgetting herself. And as the classroom of teenagers laughed at her, she decided teenagers might even laugh at a bad train wreck.

As she marched him down the hallway to the same principal, Joe Willie explained what had happened. And she nodded her head, "I know that it wasn't your fault. But we can't have you in a room full of 'spensive machines."

At age eighteen, Joe Willie was six feet tall and weighed one hundred and ninety pounds, and he felt silly being marched down the hall by Mrs. Allen, who was almost a foot shorter and a hundred pounds lighter. "That's what I tried to tell him, Mrs. Allen," Joe Willie told her.

When they got to the principal's office, Mrs. Allen tried to explain, but the new man refused to believe her. So Mrs. Allen, who was absolutely certain her machines must be protected above all else, got madder and madder. "Show him, Joe Willie!"

"Aw, now wait a minute, Mrs. Allen," Joe Willie moaned, "I don't want to . . ."

"Don't you sass me, Joe Willie Kolander!" Mrs. Allen yelled.

And as fate would have it there was a ceiling fan right above the principal's head, operating at high speed in the early September heat. So Joe Willie, becoming as exasperated as the teacher, gazed at the fan lazily and grunted, "Ah-h-harrumph." A blade from the fan came loose, crashed through the window of the office, and landed outside on the campus.

The principal became a believer, but he didn't like Joe Willie too much and wanted to punish him every time something broke; so Joe Willie pointed out one day how pretty the principal's little red Ford looked in the teachers' parking lot. "You wouldn't dare . . ." the principal said.

"If I did," Joe Willie shrugged, "you wouldn't know for sure, would you?"

The principal left him alone after that.

Joe Willie's problem with machines was a constant embarrassment to his parents and became especially traumatic for his father, the rich mechanic. A father wants to share his work with a son, but Mr. Kolander came to understand that he couldn't do that. It was sheer folly to take little Joe Willie to a new drilling site in Karankawa County, for example, because cables would break, traveling blocks would crash to the rig deck, and gasoline engines would malfunction. If they got to the site *at all*, that is, because it was more likely Mr. Kolander's truck would quit on the way.

Then there were the things Mrs. Kolander had to endure because of Joe Willie. She had to keep her washing machine in the garage, none of the clocks in the house worked, and the Kolanders couldn't take vacations together in the family car.

They were good people, but very frustrated. "What good is it to be rich, Mama?" Mr. Kolander asked his wife frequently. "What good is it to pile money in the bank if we can't buy machines?" Mr. Kolander wanted a Cadillac in the worst way.

It was a sad thing, indeed, that the Kolanders could not show off their wealth in the acceptable, and even *expected,* ways of rich Karankawa Countians. The car-buying craze of the fifties slipped by without them purchasing more than the single '51 Chevrolet—a bland, practical automobile—because Joe Willie's father refused to do otherwise.

"A yard full of Cadillacs and Lincolns? What for? So the boy can wreck them? I would even be happy if he were *normal* and had *normal* wrecks on the highway like other boys." Mr. Kolander became bitter as he grew older and couldn't properly spend his oil royalties.

Joe Willie was an excellent student, but a social flop for the most part. The other kids liked him, but he could never go on dates, and that set him apart from his peers. He could never go out with a girl because of the car problem. He could go to movies as long as he didn't glance toward the projection booth, but he had to walk downtown to the Strand Theater on Main Street. And most Karankawa County girls were more interested in riding in an expensive automobile than walking with Joe Willie. The ones willing to walk, he learned, weren't the ones he wanted to walk with.

He was a good athlete and loved to play football, but he couldn't go on any of the road trips because the bus would break down. It was easier for the high school coach to leave him at home.

So Joe Willie learned to live pretty well alone and within himself at an early age. It became natural for him, the only world he knew, and he never minded too much. He always had animals—and books.

His love for animals seemed to be a natural outgrowth of his problem with machines. Before he was eight years old, his folks realized they were going to have to make special arrangements for him. Just getting him to school every day was a major problem which couldn't be solved with the family car or the school bus. They tried a bicycle, but he never learned to ride it because it wouldn't stay in one piece long enough. So he walked to school, and his parents learned that a half-mile wasn't so hard for a little boy who was willing. And by then he had a small black dog, called Blackie, that went with him.

Then, after his eighth birthday, his father gave him the greatest gift he would ever receive, a horse named Big John. Big John was tall, red, and gentle, and became Joe Willie's best friend. He rode Big John to school every day for almost ten years, staked him in a vacant lot nearby while he was in class, and rode him home in the afternoon. Big John and Blackie taught Joe Willie about his special affinity for animals.

He learned that he, his horse, and the ugly dog shared a kind of mental telepathy. In the back of the Kolander home, where Joe Willie's father spent long, happy hours planning and building a large barn for the horse, Big John lived in a fenced two-acre pasture. After the first week of being ridden to school, Joe Willie and his parents noticed, the horse stood next to the pasture gate, waiting to be fed and saddled each morning.

"Of course he stands and waits," Mr. Kolander told his wife, "because he knows it's time for breakfast. He's a real eater, that horse."

But Joe Willie came to know it was more than that. On weekends at mid-day, or late on cool evenings, or whenever Joe Willie decided to take a ride, he knew all he had to do was sit inside the house and *think* about it. And invariably Big John would be standing before the gate when Joe Willie walked out the back door.

He told his mother about it one Saturday morning.

"P-sshaw!" said Joe Willie's practical mother. "The horse is only hungry, your father said so."

Normally, in the solid, Dutch Protestant home, that would have been the end of it. For whatever father said was as surely true as the Stone Tablets in the Old Testament. But Joe Willie was adamant.

"Pick a time," the eight year old firmly told his mother.

"What do you mean?"

"*You* watch the horse. Wait till he is far back in the pasture. Then *you* come and tell me when to ride. I'll be in my room reading."

Three hours later, in the heat of the Texas morning, Mrs. Kolander told Joe Willie, "The horse is standing asleep near the back fence. Call him in your mind."

Joe Willie nodded, put away the Zane Grey book his teachers were certain he could not read, and pulled on his boots. "Come on, Mama, Big John is standing beside the gate."

And the horse was there, looking over the gate with his short, red ears pointed toward the back door as Joe Willie and his mother came out.

Mrs. Kolander looked at her son with sadness in her eyes. "You are a strange child, Joe Willie Kolander. I love you will all the heart that is in me. But you are a strange child."

Joe Willie walked to the spacious and clean barn, dragged the heavy saddle from its place in the tack room, and climbed up on the platform his father had built for him. He was too short to saddle the horse from the ground. When he was ready he nodded at Big John, and the horse walked up beside the platform and waited for the child to saddle him.

Joe Willie rode northwestward when he reached the edge of Karankawa City, toward Brand's Bayou, and the small black dog trotted behind him.

If one looks at Karankawa City, Texas, today, it is exceedingly hard to imagine a child roaming its streets and highways on the back of a big horse. Great freeways pass it on two sides, broad highways bisect it between the freeways, and there is heavy traffic in most parts of the city. Shopping malls cover what used to be salt marshes; churches vie for the attention of prospective converts in residential areas that were once dairy farms; neat homes on manicured, fifty-foot lots of St. Augustine grass testify to the aspirations, attitudes, and limits of hard-hatted refinery workers consumed by the American Dream. And in the two-block span of Main Street in "Old Town"—the total extant business district when Joe Willie was young—aging merchants, barbers, and drugstore coffee drinkers still heatedly discuss the faults of local labor unions ("the damned common-

ists") and severely criticize the methods and intelligence of the Karankawa High football coach. Some things never change.

And today, as in 1950 when Joe Willie was in high school, the
old men only whisper about Joe Willie's problem, and regard him
as people might note a retarded child grown to a retarded manhood
amongst them. They seem to feel a certain guilt by association, as
if they were touched and tainted by his having attained adulthood
in Karankawa County, and their rare references to his lonely life
on Brand's Bayou are often couched in tepid resentment of his very
being.

Brand's Bayou angles down from the northwest corner of Karankawa County, meanders through great marshes, through occasional
oak thickets wherever its banks rise high enough above the marsh
to sustain them, and joins the Neches River near Sabine Lake. Joe
Willie first began riding Big John to the copse of oaks and hack-
berries beside Brand's Bayou on the morning his mother told him
of his "strangeness."

He rode slowly, looking closely at the profusion of grass growing
all around him when he passed the Karankawa City Limit sign and
entered the broad fenced prairie he knew had belonged to his family for generations. He listened to the wind. It was a ride of some
fifteen miles, a mere afternoon of mild exercise for Big John. The
cattle trail he rode twisted, turned, and followed the path of least
resistance established by cattle almost a century before. It was on
that trip that he first saw the cabin beside the bayou, standing beneath oak limbs hung with Spanish moss. He was enthralled by its
forlorn beauty.

He sat on Big John and let his eyes drink in the quiet dignity
of the old cow camp. Its boarded sides were weatherbeaten to a soft
grayness that revealed grain patterns; the tin roof was rusted through
in spots and an old concrete cistern leaned unevenly beside the house
on creosoted timbers long since rotted through. Yellow-red flowers
sprouted from weeds randomly scattered about what had once been
a yard, and the soft voices of doves drifted from somewhere in the
distance. Brand's Bayou moved silently past some fifty yards away,
ten feet below the bluff where the cow camp stood.

He returned often after that. He was only a child back then, but there were few people in Karankawa County and little traffic danger, and his father was prominent. Everyone who saw Joe Willie astride the big horse knew who he was and they kept his parents apprised of his whereabouts. It would have been impossible for him to get lost.

And, although they never spoke of it, Mr. and Mrs. Kolander came to enjoy Joe Willie's trips to the cow camp as much as he did. His absence meant they could drive the car to town, his mother could shop, and his father could walk unfettered about the small business district. Whenever Joe Willie wasn't along, things were easier for Mr. Kolander. He could relax his vigil over the boy's roving eye and not worry what effect a passing glance might have on parked cars, a revolving barber pole, or the soda fountain at the corner drugstore. So when Joe Willie wanted to ride to Brand's Bayou, his parents usually agreed.

After Joe Willie's love for the place became apparent, his father sent a crew to build a new fence around the property—several miles of fence, altogether—and he personally repaired the old house. In time, Joe Willie was allowed to spend weekends there with Robert Earl, an elderly black man to whom the Kolanders came to entrust his care. By the time Joe Willie was fourteen, he stayed for weeks at a stretch on Brand's Bayou. At sixteen, he spent his whole summer vacation there, and that became the rule throughout his high school years. He left home when school was out in May and didn't return till after Labor Day in September.

Robert Earl didn't know his own age, but he had worked for two generations of Kolanders; three, if Joe Willie was counted. His job had always been the care of Kolander cattle, and Mr. Kolander transferred him to the Brand's Bayou pasture only after Joe Willie showed an interest in it. Before that, the elder Kolander didn't think a cowhand was necessary there; it was near enough to oversee himself and he had few cattle at Brand's Bayou.

But practicality surfaced when he moved Robert Earl from the other job. "We can't have him with nothing to do but watch over the boy." So Mr. Kolander moved five hundred head of cattle along with Robert Earl. When the cattle were turned into the pasture, he looked at the whole operation with satisfaction. He now had his son, his cowhand, and many cattle located in the same spot. It quenched his Dutch desire for unity, function, and tidiness.

Robert Earl carried himself with dignity and Joe Willie liked him immediately. He was tall, his brown skin the same texture as the leather on Joe Willie's saddle, and he spoke slowly and deliberately. His graying hair and the wrinkles about his dark eyes added distinction to his demeanor. He was illiterate, but his deep voice suggested keen reflection on subjects with which he was familiar, and he looked upon Joe Willie as a sacred trust.

School vacations, summertime, and weekends eventually became the times Joe Willie Kolander lived for, during his high school years. He was comfortable with Robert Earl, and the older man was happy without all the modern conveniences of town living. They drew water from the well beside the cow camp by hand with rope and bucket, cooked on a wood stove, and the boy read by candlelight. Joe Willie's father had sent kerosene lanterns at first, but even those wouldn't function correctly with Joe Willie around. The little handles used to regulate the flow of fuel to the flame kept breaking off. And the manually operated can openers Robert Earl was accustomed to using had to be eliminated—they wouldn't work either. So they opened cans of fruit and vegetables with a butcher knife; Robert Earl's pocketknife refused to stay in one piece almost immediately, and the old gentleman shook his head in awe of Joe Willie's problem.

"You got the powah," Robert Earl told Joe Willie every time the simplest machine broke down in the boy's presence. "You is really got the powah."

Joe Willie disagreed. "It's not power, Robert Earl, it's more like a curse."

"Ain't no curse. Ain't no voodoo 'cause you is a good chile, Joe Willie. You jes' got the *powah.*"

They worked together, ate together, and slept in the same room of the cow camp. Robert Earl taught Joe Willie the psychology of cows and the traits of the multitude of animals that lived in the marshy pasture. "Animals be steady takin' care of *theyselfs.* Ain't got no time for mischiefs and foolishness. Muskrat happy in water, fiel'-mouse happy in the fiel', and bobwhite quail happy with his covey.

The win' blow and water run. Grass grow and cows eat. Animals happy jes' takin' care of theyselfs."

Joe Willie was fascinated. He had his father and mother buy books on the plants and animals around him, and in time he became a naturalist; expert on the flora and fauna of his surroundings. He came to savor each day's common happenings, and he and Robert Earl discussed them in rich detail every night. They spoke of how a certain cow walked with a peculiar hitch in her step; how alligators in Brand's Bayou eased through the muddy water without making a ripple; how there were some weeds cattle would eat, and the way mosquitoes appeared three days after rain. Robert Earl sat and listened in respectful quiet when Joe Willie read passages on nature, and he nodded in solemn agreement when he learned that mosquito eggs can lie dormant, only to hatch after years of drouth.

By the time Joe Willie graduated, he and Robert Earl had switched roles. Joe Willie became the teacher, Robert Earl the pupil. And they were fast friends who often found no need to talk. In moments when both sat on the cow camp porch and watched a multicolored sunset, there seemed no need for words.

Joe Willie wanted to attend college, but he knew his problem wouldn't allow him to. So after graduation he made the permanent move that was inevitable, and the old cow camp became his home. There was little to be done in the transfer of his personal things; most of them he had moved already. The physical aspect of moving was easily accomplished. He felt a temporary sadness in leaving, and his mother shed a few tears, but his final departure was a simple thing. He mounted Big John and rode away as he had done hundreds of times before, avoided long glances at passing automobiles, and arrived at the cow camp before dark.

Mr. and Mrs. Kolander visited him often at first, then their visits became fewer and fewer until a ritual was established. They came by on the first Sunday of each month to bring supplies and ask what he would need on their next visit. It wasn't feasible, of course, for them to drive to the house or park too near the pasture gate for Joe Willie to unload the supplies from the back of his father's truck. They had to unload, drive a half-mile down the road, walk back, and wait for their son to appear. Mr. Kolander found it especially tedious when Joe Willie's supplies included a box of heavy books, which was often the case. "I'm getting old, Joe Willie," Mr. Kolander said, "I might have to get someone else to bring these heavy books to you."

So it came to pass that Joe Willie Kolander's parents only came to see him on holidays or his birthday. The monthly supplies were brought by one of his father's hired hands, who dumped the load at the gate and left, and Joe Willie was without human contact, except for Robert Earl.

In the five years after Joe Willie left home, the Kolanders never admitted to each other that they were happier than they had been since Joe Willie was born. But Mr. Kolander bought the long-desired Cadillac, Mrs. Kolander moved her washer inside the house, and the clocks functioned again. They began to take long trips in the car and felt as if they had finally been released from an extended prison sentence.

They were on a trip to San Antonio, in bright midday under a Texas sun, when a train crushed the Cadillac and Kolanders into an unrecognizable heap near Cuero, Texas. The railroad warning signal had failed, and neither Kolander saw the train as they lounged in deep, Cadillac comfort.

Joe Willie rode an aging Big John to the double funeral services at the cemetery and tried to avoid glancing at the parked cars all around him. The mortuary people had the foresight to have the Kolander coffins lowered by hand, not trusting the automatic mechanism with Joe Willie around. The funeral director was a native of Karankawa County and knew of Joe Willie's problem.

There were no trees at the cemetery, and Joe Willie stood in bright sunlight and watched morosely as forever-fused pieces of Kolander and Cadillac were buried beneath Karankawa County's flat coastal plain. They were at one with their machine, Joe Willie thought, and he remembered reading how Indians were sometimes buried with their favorite horse. But he felt this was somehow different.

"Three machines," Joe Willie whispered to Robert Earl as they stood beside the graves after the others were gone. "A train signal, a car, and a train. Three machines . . . and I wasn't even there."

In cash, Joe Willie inherited eight million dollars; in real estate, twenty thousand acres; and in producing oil wells, twenty-six. He was the only heir, and the Kolander lawyer was forced to suffer the pain and indignity of visiting the cow camp to explain it to him.

The lawyer, Mr. Brooks, sweated through his suit and removed his tie as he rode a Kolander cow pony the eight miles from the pasture gate to the old house. His suede shoes barely reached the stirrups, and he bounced along the rough trail and clutched a tan briefcase next to his thin chest. Joe Willie looked at Robert Earl and grinned as they rode on either side of him.

"I'm glad you could come," Joe Willie sat easily in the saddle and talked to the lawyer. "We don't get many visitors."

The lawyer nodded, tried an unsuccessful smile, and grimly held on to the briefcase. Every trotting step of the cow pony slammed his testicles against the saddle, and for the life of him, he couldn't figure how to protect them with one cupped hand, hang on to the leather case, and hold the reins too. When Joe Willie helped him off the pony at the cow camp, Mr. Brooks could hardly stand.

They made the arrangements for the disposition of Joe Willie's inheritance. Mr. Brooks would visit the cow camp monthly for Joe Willie to sign papers, make decisions, and order supplies. Beyond that, Brooks was in charge. And he wasn't entirely certain the money he received from the Kolander estate was worth a monthly pony ride to the cow camp.

As far as Joe Willie was concerned, the arrangement was satisfactory. Outside of books, more bookcases to keep them, a few clothes, and the staples of living, he and Robert Earl didn't need much. He was happy working the cattle, tending his horses and the pack of cur-dogs he had accumulated, and watching the wild animals around him.

But the good Karankawa City people were appalled.

"Ain't that just the way of it?" asked an unemployed, would-be entrepreneur in Murphy's pool hall. "A half-wit kid who ain't smart enough to handle a wheelbarrow. And *he* inherits millions. There ain't no justice in this world."

The men sitting around Murphy's domino table nodded in solemn agreement, in the manner of men accustomed to discussing high finance, then returned to the spots arrayed before them. The fifty cents each had wagered on the game represented more than a half-can of beer.

The president of the Karankawa County State Bank looked over
the Kolander account, nudging half a million dollars, and cursed
Joe Willie silently when he thought of the other seven-point-five
million scattered in banks across Texas.

Miss Effie Tyndol bemoaned the loss of the elder Kolanders to
the cultured, blue-haired ladies of her Karankawa Garden Club.
"They was such fine people," Miss Effie told the group, "and so . . .
burdened. Why they's just no burden like havin' a afflicted child. And
that's all they are to it."

Then Miss Effie sipped tea with a white-gloved pinky finger raised
as she looked at the Karankawa Garden Club through her bifocals.
And she dreamed of silver-haired millionaire gentlemen in double-
breasted, navy blue suits with bright-colored family crests emblazoned on their pockets.

"Joe Willie Kolander deserves all that money about as much as
his mangy, red horse," the young lawyer, Brooks, told his bride of
two years, as they lay cold together in their conjugal bed. "An old
man and cow shit; that's all Joe Willie's interested in." And lawyer
Brooks dreamed of Las Vegas whores and neon until he slept that
night. Once asleep, he had nightmares about swollen testicles, and
a giant who kept hitting Brooks' manhood with hot, red lights—
from astride an elephant-sized horse.

In the Karankawa City Barber Shop, the barber, who had long
ago been a cheerleader for the local team, explained to his customers
how the football coach was a fool. "He left Joe Willie *home* when
the team was on the road." The barber waved a razor as he spoke.
"If he had only *cultivated* Joe Willie . . . Why, he could even have
built us a new football stadium."

The three barber shop regulars sighed at the barber's deep knowledge of football, local politics, and the coach's abysmal lack of foresight. They dreamed of long, green vistas of rich Bermuda grass upon
which gold-uniformed Karankawa High players won state champion-
ships, and they saw themselves gloating to less fortunate chemical
plant co-workers from nearby towns.

In the years that followed, Joe Willie Kolander suffered more
trauma. Big John died at the ripe age of twenty-six, an ancient and
much-beloved animal that Joe Willie felt would be irreplaceable de-

spite the millions available to buy more horses. Joe Willie himself
dug a grave for Big John, unwilling to leave the body of his old friend
to the tender mercies of roving wolves and other night animals.

Then Robert Earl died in his sleep one night. He was very old
and hard put to mount his horse every morning. It was fitting, Joe
Willie thought, because Robert Earl had long ago decided he didn't
want to live if he couldn't ride the marshes and look at the cattle.
"Be better if a young hoss kick my brains out," Robert Earl said,
"than to lay up in a bed. Wuthless and blind."

The few people in Karankawa County's black community were
tolerant of Joe Willie's wishes in the burial of Robert Earl. His body
was loaded in a wagon pulled by a matched pair of bright sorrel
horses, bought for the occasion with Kolander money, and the pro-
cession of mourners walked or rode horseback to the cemetery. It
was a hot summer day, and Joe Willie smiled when he heard the
soft voices of doves through the respectful silence of those gathered to observe Robert Earl's passing. And he was at ease as he
looked around him at the solemn, black faces, heard the stamping
of hooves, and smelled earthy horse-smells. It was seemly, he thought,
and natural.

He was alone now. He lost himself in work on the ranch, read
voraciously, and even subscribed to a Houston newspaper. He rode
a horse the seven miles to the pasture gate each morning before
daylight, picked up the newspaper, and read it when the sun rose
in the east. He kept up with all that happened in the world. And
when he learned of the invention of some new machine and read
the glowing reports of how it would benefit mankind, he smiled
softly and shook his head in wonder.

Decades passed and Joe Willie stayed in the pasture alone except
for the monthly visits of the lawyer. Brooks, being only a few years
older than Joe Willie, grew rich from the Kolander account and dutifully made the bone-jarring trip regularly. But affluence didn't change
his aversion to his client and his client's life-style. Despite Joe Willie's
obvious grasp of world affairs and ability to make good decisions
about the administration of the Kolander fortune, Brooks looked
upon him as backward and dull. He too saw the Kolander fortune
as wasted on a half-wit.

Wars were fought and men walked on the moon. The world depleted its resources at an alarming rate and presidents were shot. The intelligence of men was randomly replaced by "artificial intelligence," oil prices fluctuated wildly, causing painful unemployment in Karankawa County, and Joe Willie Kolander was largely unaffected as he grew to middle age in his cabin beside Brand's Bayou. The thousands of acres in the Kolander pasture effectively insulated him from the world, and the Kolander millions guaranteed that he could remain so.

Then one morning, when his hair was gray and he was a few weeks shy of his fiftieth birthday, he found several dead birds, saw the white bellies of dead fish float by in the brown water, and came upon some sick cattle. He was mystified, at first, then decided that perhaps the common denominator was to be found in the bayou's water. He rode upstream a few miles until he came to the barbed wire fence which marked the north boundary of his pasture. He saw nothing amiss until his eyes followed the course of Brand's Bayou northwestward to the horizon. There he saw the ugly smokestacks of Tex-Eco-Safe Chemical Company rise sharply against the distant sky. He quickly looked away, fearing the destruction his steady gaze might cause, then he rode back to his home with a firm set to his jaw.

Tex-Eco-Safe, as it was called by hundreds of Karankawa Countians who worked there, made the ingredients for Agent Orange, Joe Willie knew from reading the sycophantic account in the newspaper. During the Vietnam War Agent Orange was used as a defoliant in Southeast Asian jungles, and many American soldiers exposed to it developed cancer in the years following that conflict. Southeast Texans were proud to be part of such a patriotic effort, and their pride was reflected in newspaper reports of the chemical's effectiveness. Joe Willie Kolander knew technology had finally caught up with him; Tex-Eco-Safe Chemical was killing his animals.

Several days later, on lawyer Brooks's visit to the cow camp, Joe Willie told him of his suspicion. "I want it stopped," Joe Willie said, "and I don't mean in a few days or a month. I want it stopped *now*."

"Joe Willie," Brooks spoke condescendingly, as if he were talking to a retarded child. "You don't understand. Tex-Eco-Safe is vital to the interests of America and to the progress of Karankawa County.

77

They're a multinational company with more money than you can imagine. You cannot simply tell them to stop. Besides, you're not sure it's their fault your animals are dying."

"I'm sure," Joe Willie answered, "and I'll tell you something else, Brooks. If you don't go see them today, I'll get me another lawyer."

Brooks shrugged helplessly. "It'll be as you say, Joe Willie."

"Good," Joe Willie smiled, "and when you get their answer you can ride back out here and let me know."

"You mean . . . *today?*"

"Damned right, Brooks," Joe Willie nodded, "today."

It was after dark when the lawyer finally appeared at Joe Willie's pasture gate, and he was happy to see Joe Willie waiting for him. He had hoped he wouldn't have to make another ride to the cow camp.

"They refused to even discuss it with me," Brooks said, "except to say it just wasn't *possible* that they were responsible for the death of your animals."

"I see." Joe Willie rubbed the neck of the saddled horse beside him. "Okay. I'll tell you what, Brooks, you get me one of those newspaper folks here tomorrow. I've got a story to tell."

"I advise you not to do that, Joe Willie. Your accusation against them is unsubstantiated, you can't prove it. They'll sue you for everything you own."

"So what's the difference, Brooks? Whether they kill off everything I care about or sue me for all I own? I lose either way, don't I?"

"But all that money . . ." Brooks began.

"Screw the money! You get me a reporter or you can forget any more Kolander money!"

The lawyer had never seen Joe Willie so angry, and he hurried away as quickly as possible. He called the reporter, a young man named Farris Henry, and begged him to see Joe Willie Kolander. "I'll *pay* you to go," Brooks whined, and Farris Henry agreed.

"I figure I'm some kind of mutant," Joe Willie told the young reporter as they sat inside the cow camp. "I'm the result of a built-in gene that's been around a long time, just in case it was needed."

Farris Henry looked at Joe Willie through worried eyes. Here I am, the journalist thought, seven miles from the nearest road, with a damned horse my only means of escape, and I'm talking to a man

78

who's obviously deranged. But, being the thorough reporter he was, Henry clicked on the tape recorder in his pocket. He figured he could at least get a good story of a deranged hermit, if the Tex-Eco-Safe thing didn't prove out.

Joe Willie grinned broadly and told Farris Henry, "You might as well put that damned thing up. It won't work."

"Sure it will," Henry's smile was broad too, "I just bought it last week."

"Turn it off and lay it on the kitchen table there," Joe Willie said.

Henry did, and Joe Willie gazed at it for ten seconds. "Now turn it on, son. And watch the tape ooze out of it."

When Farris Henry turned the tape player on again, he could only watch in horror as the tape squirted through the tiny slits in the plastic.

"Now I know you've heard stories of bionic men; seen them on television, I expect, like most everybody in this country. And you can halfway accept that, because everybody else does. You figure artificial limbs, artificial hearts, and artificial intelligence in computers makes such bionics feasible in the near future. Isn't that right?"

Farris Henry had not yet gotten past the pile of worthless tape lying before him on Joe Willie's kitchen table, and his composure was badly shaken. He nodded dumbly at Joe Willie, took out a pad and pencil, and began taking notes.

"So why not the opposite of that? What if someone like me is needed to curb the power machines have over us? What if I'm only the first of a long line of people designed by nature to protect us from machines? And from organizations like Tex-Eco-Safe Chemical? Is that any harder to believe than a plastic heart?"

"Uh, I dunno," Farris Henry said as he wrote furiously. "I just don't know."

So it was that Joe Willie told a skeptical reporter his life story and explained his suspicions about Tex-Eco-Safe Chemical. "I'm told," Joe Willie said at the end of his narration, "that companies like Tex-Eco-Safe are examples of 'progress.' And that may very well be true. But progress for whom? I submit such 'progress' will lead to the destruction of our environment if left alone and unsupervised, and I further submit that our governmental entities won't interfere—except in a very superficial way—with the operation of plants like

Tex-Eco-Safe. I fear we individual citizens will have to act on our own to stop the poisoning of our homes, neighborhoods, and cities. That's why I sent for you."

"You expect *me* to accuse Tex-Eco-Safe Chemical of pollution?" Farris Henry asked.

"No," Joe Willie answered quickly, "of course not. I only want you to print *my* accusations. I may not exactly be everyone's idea of a public-spirited citizen, but most people in this county know who I am, I expect. And I'm not without resources. I estimate my family's estate is close to a hundred million dollars by now, so I think someone will listen."

"And if they don't?"

"Then we'll go from there," Joe Willie grinned.

Farris Henry printed the article containing Joe Willie's accusation. He included a description of Joe Willie, his home on Brand's Bayou, and an account of his life. Nothing happened. Tex-Eco-Safe Chemical didn't even bother to answer Joe Willie's charges, and the local environmental people read the story with morning coffee and condescending chuckles. Lawyer Brooks gritted his teeth and waited for the inevitable lawsuit; aging Karankawa Rotarians cursed Joe Willie for hurting the county's chances to "attract new industry" and whispered to each other about his mental retardation. At Murphy's pool hall the descendants of earlier domino players cursed Joe Willie for casting aspersions upon "one of the few successful bidnesses left in this county." And nothing happened.

Joe Willie gave it two weeks, and during that time he rode the marshes and prairies of the Kolander pasture with a vengeance. He found more dead animals: birds, armadillos, rabbits, possums, and a few calves. He sent for Farris Henry once more.

"Tell 'em again," he said. "And this time tell 'em if something isn't done . . . Well, tell 'em I'll take care of it myself if need be."

"But what can you do?" Henry asked.

"You just tell 'em."

So Farris Henry once more told them in his newspaper. And once again nothing happened.

Two weeks later, on a moonless night, Joe Willie Kolander took the barbed wire loose from his north fence line and rode his horse into the adjacent pasture. He guided the horse along the bank of

Brand's Bayou until he was within a quarter-mile of Tex-Eco-Safe Chemical Company, and he stared at a fleet of eighteen-wheeled trucks clustered together in a well-lighted parking lot. "Ker-boom!" Joe Willie said to the fleet of trucks.

On the truck nearest him, the engine mounts slipped loose and the huge diesel fell to the asphalt below. The truck aligned in front of it suffered eighteen flat tires, and two others would never again function without a major overhaul because of warped pistons.

It was enough, Joe Willie thought, so he turned his horse and rode slowly home. He had meant it as only a show of strength.

The authorities at the chemical company were patently contemptuous of life on this planet, but they were far from stupid. It was plain that Joe Willie Kolander had destroyed their trucks with malice aforethought. Indeed, he had even *advertised* that he would do so. They reported what they termed "wanton destruction of private property" to the Karankawa County Sheriff, Little Boy Jefferson, and that gentleman sent Deputy Ragsdale to question Joe Willie at the cow camp. Which was, of course, somewhat more difficult than Deputy Ragsdale—or "LBJ," as the sheriff was fondly called by many of his constituents—had expected. The "road" to the cow camp was rough, and that was just the first of Deputy Ragsdale's problems.

The unit Deputy Ragsdale drove (all the deputies in Karankawa County were sagely taught to call county cars "units") was not a new model. The deputy had entered the pasture gate and driven less than a mile toward Joe Willie's home when his unit got hopelessly mired in marsh mud. He radioed for help and LBJ himself responded. And upon surveying the situation with experienced eyes, LBJ told Deputy Ragsdale, "You're undoubtedly dumber'n I thought to drive out here in your unit through this goddamned marsh."

Ragsdale glanced at the sheriff's unit, parked directly behind his own, and remained silent. Little Boy Jefferson was six feet, nine inches tall, and to argue with him was futile.

"What we gotta do, you silly sumbitch, is call for the Sheriff's Posse to brang horses."

LBJ was secretly elated. It was all too seldom he had an opportunity to apprehend a subject (all Karankawa County sheriff's deputies were taught to call people they questioned "subjects") on horseback in the grand tradition. He got on the radio in his unit immediately. "Maureen," he told the central operator at the Sheriff's Department in Karankawa City, "we got a real problem here. Ragsdale's got his goddamned unit buried up in the marsh. What we gonna need is a HR-15XL, you got that now, Maureen?" (All deputies were told to use codes whenever possible.)

"HR-15XL?" Maureen asked. "What's that?"

"Jesus Christ, Maureen," LBJ yelled, "look it up in your code book. I'm busy as a tom cat coverin' shit out here."

Maureen did as she was told. But when she looked up the meaning of HR-15XL, saw that it was a call for the posse, and broadcast it to the county's units, she had no idea that *all* the deputies would respond. Eight trucks pulling loaded horse trailers descended upon the Kolander pasture, dutifully followed the tracks of LBJ's and Ragsdale's units, and made the century-old cow path completely impassable. Only the first three arrived safely behind LBJ's unit; the rest bogged in blue mud.

Excited as boys playing cowboys and undaunted by the mud, the mired deputies unloaded horses and rode pell-mell through the marsh to reach LBJ's side.

"Where the goddamned hell is *my* goddamned horse?" LBJ roared at the riders as they skidded to a halt all around him. "You sumbitches think I'm gonna *walk?*"

The deputies looked around them as if expecting to find LBJ's horse trotting up any second. "Well, *hail*, LBJ," a mud-besmattered Deputy Crawford said, "Maureen just broadcast a damned HR-15XL, she didn't say to brang your hoss. We didn't know . . ."

LBJ had had the presence of mind to count deputies as the man spoke. "*And who the hell's mindin' the damned store?* We got ever' deputy—ever' goddamned unit—rat chere in this here marsh. I bet the criminals is havin' a field day!"

Two deputies began counting heads, pointing their fingers as they counted, just to make sure LBJ was correct. The rest looked around at each other sheepishly.

LBJ pointed to deputy Crawford. "I'll tell you what we gonna do. You get off from *pawn* that horse." He indicated four other deputies with an enormous fist: "You four get the hell back on duty, and Ragsdale, you and Crawford stay here with the damned units. It'll take us at least a *are* to ride out there and a *are* to ride back; we can't leave Karankaway County to tend its-own-self."

Joe Willie was sitting on his front porch rubbing the long ears of a cur-dog when LBJ and three deputies rode up to his house on sweaty horses. The five other dogs lying about the porch began to bark furiously at the strangers, and Joe Willie stepped off the porch. He quieted the dogs and stood looking at the entourage silently.

"You Joe Willie Kolander?" LBJ asked.

"That's not the question," Joe Willie told the sheriff of Karankawa County. "The question is who are you and what the hell are you doin' on my property?"

"I'm the sheriff, and I want to ast you some questions."

"You generally bring that much help to ask questions?" Joe Willie smiled.

LBJ sat on Deputy Crawford's dun horse and looked down at Joe Willie. "You kind of a smart-ass, ain't you boy?"

"What's your question?" Joe Willie ignored the sheriff's provocation.

"Tex-Eco-Safe Chemical thinks you destroyed some o' their trucks last night. Did you?"

"Yep," said Joe Willie Kolander, "I sure's hell did."

"Then you're gonna have to come with me," LBJ said.

"Naw, I don't think so. What you need to do is arrest that damned chemical company for killin' my stock."

LBJ grinned wolfishly at Joe Willie. "Get a gun on him, boys. Looks like we gonna have to do this the fun way."

The deputies pulled pistols and leveled them at Joe Willie. Sheriff LBJ kept grinning. "What do you say now?"

Joe Willie riveted his eyes on the pistols, and one by one their component parts fell onto the ground around the horses' feet.

"I ain't got nothing to say," Joe Willie shrugged.

The deputies looked at Joe Willie, looked at each other, dismounted, and began picking up the various parts of their pistols. Sheriff LBJ sat astride the dun horse with his mouth open for a moment before he pointed his own pistol at Joe Willie. Seconds later he was watching the sidearm fall to pieces before his eyes.

"I heard about you," said the sheriff of Karankawa County, "but I never believed it till now."

"Good," Joe Willie was smiling again. "Now let me explain something, Sheriff. You and these boys here can wrestle me down and drag me to the highway if you want to. But when we get there, how are you gonna get me to jail? You can't take me in a car because I'll ruin it just like I did those trucks last night. You can make me walk, I suppose, but what's going to happen when we get there? Your jail won't hold me. I'll break any kind of lock you can put on the cell. You better ride on out of here and think about that a while. I'm not going anywhere, I've been here all my life and I don't expect to ever leave. If you need me, I won't be hard to find."

"I'm *bound* to arrest you," LBJ said. "It's my duty to arrest you."

"Are you willing to risk the hell I can raise by just strolling down the highway? Do you know I can walk toward town and destroy every machine between here and Karankawa City? You want to take that chance?"

LBJ was determined. "I'll *have* to take that chanc't, I ain't got no choice. The law is clear and I've got a complaint against you."

Joe Willie shrugged and looked around him. "Who's gonna take care of all these animals while I'm gone? If you arrested those criminals over at Tex-Eco-Safe, would you shut the plant down and let *it* rot?"

"That ain't got nothin' to do with this," said LBJ.

Joe Willie stood and stared at LBJ for long seconds before he spoke again. "Sheriff, I can get away from you whenever I choose. I can damned near blow up the Karankawa County Courthouse if you take me there. You like the air-conditioning system in your office? You like to work cool at your desk? Isn't it nice to have that central radio system at the Sheriff's Department? And doesn't the courthouse have a boiler to warm it in winter? Telephones? And all of those nice squad cars parked together near your office?"

LBJ sat on the dun horse in unaccustomed silence.

"And when you take me to trial, how will the court reporter, for example, make a transcript of the trial? His little machine won't work when I'm present; neither will a tape recorder. And don't we have to pass the Electric Utility Company on the way to the courthouse? You want the whole county to die because of me?"

84

"I don't believe you," LBJ said. "I don't think you can do all that."

"Okay, Sheriff," nodded Joe Willie Kolander, "I'll get my horse. I haven't been to town in almost twenty-six years; I guess it's time I visited ya'll anyway."

Joe Willie got on his horse, looked at the six-pack of dogs, and started down the trail toward the highway. The dogs trotted behind him.

"Ain't no use in you callin' them dogs," LBJ said. "We ain't got room for 'em in the units. Besides, they can't stay in the cell with you."

"Oh, we ain't gonna ride in the vehicles," Joe Willie grinned, "and we ain't gonna spend much time at the courthouse."

"We'll see about that," LBJ barked. He was regaining the confidence lost when his gun fell apart. The subject was cooperative and headed for jail.

The ride to where Deputy Ragsdale had bogged his unit was uneventful. And when the party of tired and muddy deputies and sheriff arrived, Ragsdale's unit was still stuck. He and Deputy Crawford leaned across its hood and grinned while they watched half of Karankawa County's Sheriff's Department ride up with the prisoner.

"Get the subject in my unit," LBJ ordered, "then get Ragsdale's unit unstuck. We're goin' to the courthouse."

Then, as the group looked on with unbelieving eyes, smoke began to rise from the hood of LBJ's car, and all four tires of Ragsdale's unit went simultaneously flat.

Joe Willie shifted his gaze down the cow track toward the trucks still mired, and each of them suffered similar mechanical problems.

"Get on the radio," LBJ told Ragsdale, "and get some backup units here."

None of the radios, of course, would function. And as the sun began to set, swarms of mosquitoes rose from the deep grasses of the Kolander pasture. The fat, town-raised horses of the Sheriff's Posse were lathered with sweat, and as the mosquitoes covered them they became agitated and nervous. The gray bodies of mosquitoes began to settle upon the sheriff and his deputies, hundreds of thousands of them, and the beating of their fragile wings against the evening light was audible. They rose above the earth in swiftly moving clouds. The sheriff and his men suffered them in hot, swatting discomfort, and those among them who looked upon their prisoner were startled by his serenity.

Joe Willie Kolander sat astride his marsh horse and smiled softly. The transparent mosquito wings reflected a sunset turned golden in a trick of light, and they hummed about his head like a halo of movement that never quite touched him. He seemed immune to their bites and precious few landed on his face and arms. His horse stood quietly, and the occasional swish of its tail showed disdain for the biting insects that were driving the other horses into a frenzy. The six dogs sat and looked on in tranquil silence; insects were part of their existence.

"Dammit, LBJ," Crawford yelled, "we gotta get outta here. These damned bugs is eatin' me up!"

The sheriff, who still sat on Crawford's horse, replied, "Yeah. And one of us has to walk, Crawford, and it damned sure ain't gonna be me." He turned toward the highway and the others followed. Deputy Crawford stepped gingerly along in his expensive lizard-skin boots and tried to avoid the deepest mud holes as he walked and swatted furiously at the endless swarm of insects.

There were fewer mosquitoes when they reached the highway and plodded slowly toward town. LBJ tried to flag down automobiles as they flew past in the darkness, but the cars wouldn't stop for what their drivers perceived as a rag-tag bunch of horse nuts. None of them recognized the sheriff because they were all exceeding the speed limit. As the fat horses ridden by the sheriff and his deputies sweated furiously in the wet evening heat, it soon became clear that the posse might not arrive at the courthouse intact. Two horses were already beginning to limp on sore feet made worse by the highway's concrete surface, and Deputy Crawford's breath came in ragged gasps. His feet swelled inside his boots and his face swelled from mosquito bites.

Finally, after struggling along for almost four miles on the outskirts of Karankawa City, Crawford succeeded in stopping a car. He hurried toward it as fast as his aching feet could take him, but when he stood next to it and began excitedly telling the driver to bring help, the engine began a loud clanking, sighed, and then quit.

"Sheriff," Crawford roared, "I'm gonna shoot the sumbitch if he don't quit that!"

86

"Go ahead," said a tired LBJ, "and good luck. We already tried that. He'll just break your gun down without touchin' it."

They left the hapless driver beside his ruined automobile and walked through the darkness toward lights flickering in the distance. Then suddenly, when they were near enough to see the welcome shape of houses, the lights went out and the familiar forms disappeared in darkness.

LBJ was a student of perseverance. He believed, like generations of Texas lawmen before him, that no criminal could succeed before "a man in the right who just kept coming," but his confidence began to slip. Every time they got near any sort of building that might offer help, he was thwarted by a grinning Joe Willie who sat without speaking on a horse that never tired, surrounded by dogs who seemed able to read the mind of their master.

Once, when they were seen by one of the sheriff's own units and it slowed to aid them, LBJ took hope. But it was useless. The unit's radio malfunctioned and its engine refused to work; it sat beside the highway in darkness and the only one happy about it was Deputy Crawford. He sat inside beside a brother deputy and rested. "I don't give a damn," Crawford told his friend, "if they *ever* get the subject to jail."

One by one, as they put behind them miles, wrecked automobiles, useless radios, unserviceable electronic technology, and irate citizens, the unconditioned horses fell by the wayside until Joe Willie was the only man mounted. Unhorsed deputies and their worn-out horses were strewn over blocks of downtown Karankawa City. Sheriff Little Boy Jefferson stood beside the heaving flanks of Crawford's dun and looked up at Joe Willie in total darkness. In the second before, blocks of neon had disappeared all around them and LBJ was too tired to walk the considerable distance to the courthouse. "You wasn't kiddin' was you, Kolander? You really can play hell with all this stuff the rest of us need . . . just to *survive.*"

Joe Willie nodded and spoke softly, "I sure can. But up till now, I haven't. Why don't you think about that some, Sheriff? Why do you think I waited till *now,* this particular moment, to be destructive? I promise you, I could have been doing it all my life. I was born this way."

"Tex-Eco-Safe Chemical, I suppose. Because they really did poison your place? Hell, I already knew that, Kolander, yours ain't the first complaint we've got about them and their poison. But see, that don't matter because they are one of the few plants still makin' money here, still hirin' people. What would we do without 'em? This town would dry up and blow away. That's what matters."

"Sure it matters, Sheriff. I was born and raised here; I love this town as much as you or anyone else. But what if the chemical company decides to poison more than my place—the whole town, for instance? Can you be sure there isn't Agent Orange in the ground water already?"

The sheriff of Karankawa County stood a while in deep thought. "Go on home, Kolander, and let me think on this some more."

Chemists came in the weeks that followed and tested the water in Brand's Bayou. They found alarming amounts of chemicals there, and the results of their tests were printed in Farris Henry's newspaper. Tex-Eco-Safe Chemical only received a slap on the wrist from the agencies responsible for ensuring public safety. But Joe Willie found no more than the few animals that generally died from natural causes in his rides about the pasture. He was satisfied Tex-Eco-Safe had cleaned up its act. At least for a while, anyway, until it was again possible to dispose of its waste cheaply and raise its corporate dividends a few cents. At least for as long as Joe Willie Kolander lived.

And in downtown Karankawa City, old men still whisper about Joe Willie Kolander's affliction and assure each other it's a good thing he's not actively opposing "bidness and free enterprise." Teenagers tell stories about an old gray-bearded hermit who lives in the marsh with snakes, alligators, and a pack of man-eating dogs. Their parents don't believe Joe Willie Kolander exists. But members of the Sheriff's Department in Karankawa County, sworn to secrecy about the night of humiliating defeat by a hermit, drive past the Kolander pasture gate swiftly without looking at it. Sometimes Karankawa City citizens discuss the night electricity, telephones, and automobiles failed, but they attribute it to a fly-over by UFOs.

Farris Henry often visits Little Boy Jefferson in the Karankawa County Courthouse, and sometimes they discuss whether or not Farris should print the whole truth about Joe Willie. "Naw," LBJ

88

always says, "We'd be flooded by Yankee reporters and the damned CIA. It ain't worth it, I guess. But I sometimes wonder what old Joe Willie could do with the damned Russians . . . if you could figure a way to get him over there. Maybe he could ride that old horse to the coast and catch a sailing ship . . ."

The Karankawa Rodeo

People lined the roofs and upper-floor windows on both sides of Main Street in Karankawa City, Texas. A few hardy souls, mainly teenagers and snuff-dipping young cowboys, stood on the sidewalks, and Matilda Watkins backed her fringed surrey—pulled by a gray horse—into the curb in front of the Karankawa County Courthouse to watch the preliminaries.

Matilda was, even at seventy years old, what earlier generations had called "a handsome woman." The owner of a beer joint called the Oil Patch, she was a fifth-generation native of Karankawa County and her absence from the Karankawa Rodeo, everyone agreed, would have made it a lesser event. Each year Matilda showed up at the rodeo in her surrey, and, usually drunk, drove in the rodeo parade down Main Street, then spent the day in town sipping whiskey and swapping bawdy tales with aged cronies.

Matilda's eighteen-year-old granddaughter, Mattie, was a participant in the wild cow race. And although Matilda had offered to *give* Mattie the Las Vegas trip, Mattie refused.

"It ain't the same thing, Granny Watkins," Mattie said, "and it ain't the trip either. I want to *win* the goddamned thing."

"I ought to whip your ass with a buggy whip," Matilda told her granddaughter, "for cussin' like that."

The rodeo was an annual July Fourth event in Karankawa City. Sponsored by the local chamber of commerce and Karankawa County ranchers—some of whom had recently become oil barons, like Duke Grant—it was drastically different from other modern rodeos. Where other rodeos had a producer in charge of most rodeo details, including the provision of bucking horses, bulls, steers, roping calves, and any other animals needed, Karankawa Rodeo had no such professional. Karankawans made a conscious effort to put on a show in the spirit of the origins of Texas rodeo. Stock was furnished by local ranchers, admission was free, and where most rodeos last a few hours, the Karankawa Rodeo lasted several days—and generally into the wee hours of several mornings.

Its greatest appeal to participating cowboys, some professional, some amateur, lay in its very *lack* of organization and scheduling. There was always the lure of the unknown in the Karankawa Rodeo; neither participants nor spectators knew what would happen next. Standard events, seen in rodeos everywhere, were held, but any other event dreamed up—the more likely to maim, the better—was anxiously awaited. And citizens of Karankawa City, Texas, spent each year between rodeos thinking up such calamitous sideshows.

In 1981, widely recognized in Karankawa City as the most successful rodeo year ever, the wild cow race—much to Mattie Watkins's distress—was promoted. The jockeys in this race were female, and the race was run down Main Street in Karankawa City. One city block long, the race course began at Scotty's Longhorn Saloon, ran in front of Mel's Barber Shop, passed the Karankawa County Courthouse, and ended at Bo's Gulf Service Station. The prize for the winner was a paid trip to Las Vegas and a thousand dollars cash, all furnished by Duke Grant.

And, as in most events of the Karankawa Rodeo, there was no limit on the number of contestants. Karankawa County, Texas, pastured some fifty thousand head of cattle and horses of all descriptions, so obtaining enough stock was simple.

Frog Mason, a sixty-two-year-old, crusty ex-rodeo cowboy, rancher, and a modestly oil-rich, near-millionaire in 1981, scoffed at the idea.

"Hell," said Frog, "nowadays they ain't enough tough female riders to make this a event. We'll be lucky to get three entries."

Frog was wrong.

When they first lined up the portable bucking chutes in front of Scotty's Longhorn Saloon on Main Street, ten chutes in all, it was necessary to hold four heats, then pick two riders from each heat and hold finals. A full week before the rodeo, thirty-six women had signed up for the wild cow race.

The Karankawa Chamber of Commerce met on Monday before the rodeo, and Mel Teat, owner of Mel's Barber Shop, and several other retail merchants got nervous.

"We'll have to call ambulances from Houston," Mel told the chamber, "just to hospitalize the damned *spectators*."

The attending storekeepers nodded, mumbled to each other, then looked to Duke Grant to see what his decision would be. They knew it mattered little what their opinions were: Duke would have the final say. It had always been so. In Karankawa City, Texas, people bowed to the whims of wealth. And they would, if questioned about their submission, have told their questioner Duke Grant was "a good old boy and a pillar of the community."

Duke stood to his full height of six feet in his handmade cowboy boots, took the two-dollar cigar from his lips, wrapped himself in the mantle of his unquestioned authority, flashed an angry, florid frown at Mel Teat, and belched. "Bullshit, barber! You don't care who gets skint-up, you scared of them little ole cows your-own-self."

The Karankawa Rodeo was famous for the simplicity of its regulations, and the wild cow race had but two rules. A cow couldn't win without a rider, and in the event no rider got to the finish line—Bo's Gulf Service Station—the rider who rode the farthest would win.

Matilda sat and watched the preliminaries from the seat of her surrey, and with the exception of a few minor cuts and bruises, one broken store window, and a spectator casualty, they ended without incident. The finalists were two barmaids from Beaumont; a Galveston prostitute who desperately wanted transportation to Las Vegas where she was certain to prosper; two teachers, one from Dallas's South Oak Cliff, one from Waxahachie; a pair of twelve-year-old twins from Cut 'n Shoot, Texas, whose father said they could "ride anything with hair on it"; and, much to Matilda's chagrin, Mattie Watkins.

None of them had ridden as far as Bo's Gulf Station, and the final race, by mutual agreement, had to be postponed for an hour so that the finalists could rest and receive first aid.

One of the Beaumont barmaids and the Galveston prostitute shared their medication: a fifth of Highland Mist Scotch, half of which they poured on cuts and contusions. The other half they swallowed from the bottle. The two teachers dabbed iodine on lacerated hands, sat in the shade on the courthouse lawn, and rested. Mattie Watkins, miraculously unscathed except for a bruise she was only vaguely aware of on her right hip, sat beside Matilda in Scotty's Longhorn Saloon, sipped a can of Lone Star beer, and watched the Cut 'n Shoot twins eat ice cream cones as they chased each other around Scotty's tables squealing.

"It's gonna be a long day," Matilda sighed. "Them two little Cut 'n Shoot *bastards* are tougher than the Bremmer cattle."

"I'll wear their little *asses* out," Mattie said, "you just wait."

Matilda again took up her position before the courthouse in her surrey, buggy whip in hand, to watch the final race. A red and white banner proclaiming WELCOME JULY FOURTH RODEO KARANKAWA COUNTY, TEXAS, stretched across Main Street and popped and cracked in a brisk southeast wind. The crowd cheered from the safety of rooftops and windows, Mel Teat stood in the doorway of his barber shop, and Frog Mason sat in the cab of his pickup, curbed some fifty feet in front of the portable chutes. Loudspeakers, placed strategically atop buildings, resounded with the mellow recorded voice of Eddie Arnold singing "Cattle Call."

Frog Mason, ensconced in his truck and drinking Falstaff beer as he croaked out the words along with Eddie, in the unmelodious voice that had earned him his nickname, was so wrapped in beery euphoria that he paid little attention to anything around him. A younger generation would have said Frog was mellowed out and loose. But Matilda Watkins, having known Frog for fifty years and now watching him from her position across the street in front of the courthouse, being expert in such matters, mumbled to her gray horse, "Frog's drunk on his ass."

Eddie Arnold's voice, suddenly drowned in the teeth-grinding screech of a phonograph needle being drawn across a record, was replaced by that of Buck Bailey, the local rodeo announcer. Buck's voice was practiced in tone and cadence. He had tried for a blend of the accent of movie star Ben Jonson and the sound of Rex Allen, and he had almost succeeded. Buck's accent was rich and well-drilled Texan. And Buck more than anyone else, loved the sound of it.

"Ladies and gentlemen," Buck said, "we have finally reached the climax of today's rodeo in Karankawa City, Texas, the final heat in the wild cow race. The finish line is Bo's Gulf Station, a cow can't win without a rider, and whichever lady gets closest to the finish line wins the prize money. Mr. Duke Grant will be our starter . . . and may the best man win."

The crowd tittered at Buck's joke.

Duke Grant was attired in his best Stetson hat, a tailor-made western suit complete with string tie clasped by a hand-carved, ivory steer head, and his handmade alligator boots. He stood at the middle of the bucking chutes, placed his back against the door of chute number five, and very gravely and deliberately marched off ten paces as the crowd quieted. Duke faced the chutes, raised his pistol, a real Colt .38 loaded with live bullets—Duke had decided a blank-shooting starter's pistol would somehow betray the Texas heritage of the rodeo—and fired.

Now Duke, in full cognizance of his great responsibility as race starter, and understanding the relative danger of being in front of eight recently released, wild and angry cows, had planned his escape carefully. He would simply fire the pistol in the air, then trot off to his left, to somewhere in the vicinity of where Frog Mason's pickup was parked, and get out of harm's way.

He had not, nor could he have, planned for the late arriving photographer from a Dallas newspaper. The photographer wanted a close-up picture of the South Oak Cliff school teacher as she and her bovine mount violently vacated chute number five.

So as Duke turned to run out of the way of the mad scramble of wild cows and determined women, the photographer raced toward him, camera up, and they collided in front of chute number three and fell in a tangled mass of arms, legs, camera, and loaded .38 pistol.

Anyone who has worked cows knows there is absolutely no predicting which way irate cows will run. Especially with riders on their backs, music blaring from loudspeakers, and amidst screaming people—some of whom are throwing beer and pop bottles at them.

94

The white Brahma from chute number one, ridden by the Galveston whore, turned sharply and bucked behind the cows in chutes two and three. The cow in chute two, ridden by a drunk Beaumont barmaid who screamed, "Run, baby, run!" did as she was told, except that she wheeled and deposited her rider on the sidewalk before racing through town scattering spectators. In chute three a red and white spotted Longhorn was ridden by one of the twins from Cut 'n Shoot, Texas. The bubblegum-chewing twelve-year-old, all concentration and sticking to the cow's back like a seedtick, found time to blow a gigantic pink bubble just as her mount plunged sharp hooves into the wrestling bodies of the photographer and Karankawa City's leading citizen, Duke Grant.

Close on the heels of the bubblegum chewer came the white-Brahma-riding Galveston prostitute, eyes sparkling like Las Vegas neon. And, just as her bawling cow was in mid-jump—high in the air with front legs twisted one way and rear legs the other—Duke Grant jerked away from the photographer. As Duke extricated himself and rolled away, he pulled the trigger of his pistol and the shot echoed up and down Karankawa City's Main Street.

The bullet struck the high-flying white cow just below her left ear, and she came down in an inert, nine-hundred-pound mass. The Galveston woman rode her to the ground. Despite having heard the shot, the whore refused to believe, at first, that the cow had been killed, and she sat upon the crumpled body and raked it with her spurs. Then, when realization came, she screamed at Duke Grant, "You son-of-a-bitch, you killed my cow!"

Duke, from his prone position, yelled back at her, but his words suddenly changed to a strangled cry when he tried to rise and was levelled by the flying body of the South Oak Cliff school teacher. Her black Brangus cow ran on past, encountered Frog Mason's pickup, and in a mad leaping lunge landed head first in the truck bed.

"Boom!" Duke's pistol sounded again as he wrestled, this time with both photographer and school teacher. Again his bullet found a mark, and the black cow, skull creased by its passage, sank flat in the back of Frog Mason's truck, unconscious. And Frog, still drunk, only half awake, and still humming though no longer accompanied by Eddie Arnold, started his truck and drove slowly down Main Street toward Bo's Gulf Station and the finish line. The stunned cow lay inert in the truck bed.

Chutes four and ten were vacant at the start of the race. Chutes six and seven, occupied by the other Beaumont barmaid and the Waxahachie teacher, contributed little to the race because both riders were bucked off immediately, and the riderless cows ran off into the residential district.

From chute number eight, the other Cut 'n Shoot twin rode a red cow as if she was part of its anatomy. But the cow made a hundred and eighty–degree turn, bucked, ran back past the chutes, and was last seen heading out of town with the pigtailed girl still aboard.

And out of chute number nine, Mattie Watkins emerged on a roan-colored cow that ran a full fifty yards before deciding to buck.

Matilda had been watching the action, trying to focus her attention on her granddaughter and at the same time keep a tight rein on the gray horse hitched to her surrey. But it was entirely too much to ask of a drunk, seventy-year-old woman. The violent kaleidoscope before her developed all too quickly, and her confusion became grave concern for Mattie when she heard Duke Grant's pistol boom and saw the whore's wild cow collapse.

It was at that point that Matilda waded into the fray.

Her gray buggy horse, having been nervous and fidgety throughout all the previous races, had quieted down and regained his composure during the hour-long break between preliminaries and finals. But now, as bawling and slobbering cattle raced past him, as the crowd screamed in delight, and as gunshots were fired across the street from him, his every muscle trembled in fear and excitement. He was, in the Texas vernacular, "standing on his toes."

For there was something that had escaped Matilda's memory about the horse. She had forgotten that the gray, like most Karankawa County horses, had been a "usin'" cow horse in his youth. And despite the fact that for the last ten years his only job had been to pull Matilda's surrey, he retained that cow sense gene which had been bred into his line for more than a hundred years.

So when Matilda slacked the reins and popped him smartly on the rump with the buggy whip, the cow sense gene surfaced. Matilda's purpose was to drive her surrey across the street to where Duke Grant lay, and thrash him with her whip until he dropped the .38.

96

But the gray gelding, smelling the air like a colt, recognizing the odor of scared cows, and watching as loose cattle swept by him, didn't know Matilda's purpose. He clamped strong yellow teeth on the bit in his mouth and reverted to what he was born for.

Yanking a helpless Matilda Watkins behind him, the gray horse left the courthouse curb in a full run, passed Mattie on the roan cow, and raced toward her only remaining competition, the bubble-gum-chewing Cut 'n Shoot twin.

The twin, utterly fearless as the spotted Longhorn pitched and rolled beneath her, held one hand in the air and squealed in glee, her pigtailed hair bobbing with each jump. She would, most spectators agreed, probably have won the event had it not been for Matilda's runaway surrey and Frog Mason's slow-moving truck laden with the stunned black cow.

Frog was blithely unaware of the unconscious cow in his truck as he drove away—not to escape danger, but to gain a better vantage point. Frog seldom got excited at rodeos. He had seen and participated in so many that his interest was somewhat jaded. Nevertheless, in an attempt to see the race better, he had begun a leisurely Main Street U-turn just beyond the pigtailed twin and the slobbering cow she rode. And, at the same time, Matilda's horse was in an angling run to turn the raging Longhorn back. Horse, buggy, and truck met in the middle of Karankawa City's Main Street, forming a huge V with a bucking cow and the diminutive rider in its center.

The Dallas photographer, meanwhile, enraged at his failure to get a picture of the South Oak Cliff school teacher, was determined at least to get a shot of the cow she had been riding. The cow, of course, lay unconscious in the back of Frog Mason's truck, and as Frog began his U-turn the photographer jumped into the truck bed, straddled the stunned cow, and began taking pictures of her supine body.

(It was later that night, after Frog was getting his second wind, that he heaped upon the photographer the greatest derision of which a true Texan is capable. "I knew he was stupid," Frog croaked, "because he had on low-quarter shoes and white socks.")

Fortunately, Frog was going slowly enough to stop his truck and thus avoid a full-scale collision. Matilda's buggy horse got a trace chain hung in the truck's bumper, which held him secure, and Matilda herself, mustering all the dignity possible under the circumstances, stood up in her carriage and tried to horsewhip Frog Mason through his truck window. The Dallas photographer, losing interest in the stunned cow he was sitting astride, began taking shots of Matilda as she wielded the whip.

The Cut 'n Shoot twin also lost interest. She simply stepped off the Longhorn cow trapped between buggy and truck and blew a bubble as she strolled to the sidewalk and nonchalantly watched her mount finish the race without her.

When the day's events were over, a great argument ensued. Many people thought the prize money should go to the little pigtailed twin. After all, if it hadn't been for Matilda and Frog, she might have ridden to the finish line. But careful measurement proved that Mattie Watkins had ridden some fourteen feet farther before being thrown to the pavement.

And Duke Grant was unavailable to make the final decision. Mel Teat had proved prophetic about "hospitalizing spectators," for he stood and watched, grinning, as an ambulance hauled Duke away with siren screaming and lights flashing. "Bullshit, Duke," Mel mumbled. "You scared of them little ole cows?"

In Duke's absence, democracy prevailed in Karankawa City. The group—including Frog Mason—voted the Dallas photographer the winner. Indeed, it was Frog who pointed out that the Karankawa Rodeo's simple rules didn't include a provision about one having to sign up officially to win. Nor, in spite of the fact that all the other contestants were women, did the rules say the winner *had* to be a woman.

And Mattie Watkins was satisfied. She shrugged and told Matilda (who was relieved Mattie wasn't going to Las Vegas), "I *won* the sumbitch, and that's all I ever wanted."

The Dallas photographer was the unanimous choice.

The black cow, upon regaining consciousness in the back of Frog's truck, did not pause to take bearings or decide where she was. She came alive all at once, leapt to her feet, turned around, and jumped to the ground—with the startled photographer on her back. Everyone agreed it was a miraculous thing that he held onto the rope over the cow's withers and didn't fall. He rode her through the jump, he rode her to the finish line, and he rode her on past Bo's Gulf Service Station with his camera bobbing behind him from its leather lanyard like a taillight. And the terrified cow never bucked once—she only ran, trying to put all the distance possible between herself and Karankawa City, Texas.

And the rooftop crowd cheered.

Waiting for '57

In 1957, some eight years before War Hoss Kelly was born, the Karankawa City Gator football team won the Texas class 3A State Championship. Some people, like Rip Kelly and Joe Willie Kolander, couldn't have cared less, but most Karankawa Countians held celebrations that would have done justice to V-J Day and the end of World War II. Duke Grant, for instance, had a party at his ranch house that lasted three days. He had a barrel of whiskey installed in his sumptuous home a week before the championship game was played in Karankawa City. "Old Tenny," he explained to all who attended his celebration, "imported plumb from Tennessee."

The spigot on the barrel was shaped like a hand extended for a handshake, and one had only to press the hand downward to get a shot of whiskey.

"Don't nobody go thirsty," Duke cautioned all his guests. "Just step up there and shake hands with Old Tenny."

The barrel lasted only two and a half days. In the middle of the third day, Duke's houseboy, Juan Estrada, had to order five more bottles of the Tennessee whiskey.

Juan got his orders at two o'clock on the second day of Duke's celebration. About an hour before Duke himself passed out, he told Juan, "You sumbitch, don't you let us run out of sippin' whiskey till Christmas of 1998. We won the *Texas Championship*, by God!"

Duke, of course, had nothing to do with the Gators' championship. Whether the Gators won or lost, Duke was only a spectator, but he had advertised his upcoming victory party in the *Karankawa County News* and invited the public.

There was only one stipulation in the ad: "If we win, the party's on. If they lose, the party's off." It wasn't in Duke's nature to have a party for a bunch of losers.

Most of the Karankawa Gator Booster Club members and many Gator fans attended Duke Grant's victory party, and the most avid stayed and drank Old Tenny for a full day. Nobody, except Juan Estrada, who wasn't allowed to drink, stayed the whole three days.

Immediately after the game was over, when the cheering was done and the lights turned off in Gator Stadium, the championship-hungry Gator Boosters invaded Duke's home like victorious Vikings back from a successful rape and pillage foray in a foreign land. The party was loud and rowdy. The revelers, including players' parents, drank and danced until dawn, played the game over innumerable times, congratulated each other for having such wonderful football-playing sons, and earnestly explained to Coach Tramp Majors how lucky he was to have coached their children. "Blood will tell," Duke Grant and the Gator Boosters gravely explained to Coach Majors, "blood will tell ever' damned time."

The party had wound down considerably by the next morning. The party was saved by the appearance of several senior members of the Karankawa Gator football team. Red Carlson and his team-mates showed up unexpectedly, and the Gator fans were frantic with reverent congratulations for them.

"Red on the head, like a dick on a dog!" Duke Grant screamed at Red Carlson. "Ya'll whupped on they ass! Ya'll put Karankaway County on the Texas map! Come on in this house and shake hands with Old Tenny! Red on the head, like a dick on a dog!"

Duke, in his on-again, off-again tenure as a Karankawa Gator in the mid-forties, had worked up to a third-team center position by the time he was a high school senior. He seldom got into a game, and when he did it was because the Gators were far ahead of, or far behind, their opponent. But in his telling, a listener who didn't know him might think he had been a professional. Duke Grant be-came a better high school football player with every year that passed, and he was certain he was an expert on the finer points of the game. "Come on in this house! Tell us about it!" he yelled at Red Carlson.

Red and his teammates grinned shyly, hitched up blue jeans or stuck nervous hands in their pockets, and edged toward the barrel of Old Tenny. It wasn't often adults offered them whiskey. On the contrary, during the season they would have been reported to Coach Majors for drinking. But this was a special occasion; they were the football champions of Texas, which was, in their minds, the same as being champions of the world. They were heroes before age nineteen, and there was nothing too good for them.

Mousey Kendall, the Karankawa Drugstore's pharmacist and owner, was there when the team members arrived. "I knew when those cheerleaders painted, KILL 'EM GATORS! on my display window downtown. I knew right then – like *déjà vu* – ya'll was gonna win that game. I just felt it in my *bones*."

There was no doubt in Mousey Kendall's mind that his allowing the sign on his window had led to the state championship. Mousey had played second trombone in the Gator Band before he graduated in 1942, but since then he had become a Gator football critic; and those Karankawans to whom he expounded his expertise forgot he had never participated in football. There was tolerance in their perceptions of Gator football history that extended to all Gator Boosters. In winning they were all "good old Gators," whether or not they had ever been Gators in fact. Losing, however, was something else.

Hardhat Hastings Senior sat in Duke Grant's comfortable home, held Little Hardhat – age nine – in his lap, sipped Old Tenny, and smiled at the scene before him. He patted Little Hardhat on the shoulder and whispered in his ear. "See? When you grow up, you can be a Gator too. Like Red Carlson, there."

"Red on the head, like a dick on a dog?" asked Little Hardhat in what appeared to be the innocence of childhood. But he was perfectly aware of what he was saying, and he spoke loudly enough for everyone present to hear.

The Gator fans roared at Little Hardhat's question.

"He's a chip off the old block, what can I do?" Hardhat Senior grinned proudly.

Hardhat Hastings had moved to Karankawa City in 1943 from Buzzard Roost Prairie, Texas, in the middle of the Big Thicket. He had done everything a Buzzard Roost man was supposed to do in order to prosper – joined the Baptist church, Masonic Lodge, and Ku Klux Klan – but he still couldn't make a living. Then he got a job at Tex-Eco-Safe Chemical, got married, and fathered Little Hardhat.

Karankawa County had been good to Hardhat Hastings. He was the owner of a new Chevrolet truck, a bass boat, a home on a fifty-foot lot with two mortgages, and he had made a downpayment on a fishing cabin on the river near Buzzard Roost Prairie. "I can't wait to retire," Hardhat once told Frog Mason, "so I can go back to Buzzard Roost and raise me some string beans and new potatoes."

"Whenever they made new potatoes and string beans taste like oysters and T-bone steak," Frog croaked, "I'll raise some too."

Frog could never quite get over his contempt for anything Deep East Texans liked or did.

Tramp Majors clipped Duke Grant's victory party ad from the *Karankawa County News*, folded it, and put it in his billfold. On the Monday after the championship game, he took it out and read the words: if we win, the party's on. If they lose, the party's off. He took a red pencil and underlined " . . . we win . . . they lose," then he put the clipping back in his billfold.

In the years that followed, Tramp Majors would coach in state universities across the country. Eventually he would coach three National Football league teams, but he would never forget that clipping: *we win . . . they lose.*

Remembering those words would serve him well the rest of his football life.

Twenty years later, in 1977, Mousey Kendall, Duke Grant, Hardhat Hastings, Little Hardhat, and all the diehard Gator fans were on the edge of despair. The Gators were losing and it was impossible for them to bear.

Mousey's rodent cheeks were sunken and sallow, his nervous and jerky movements became more pronounced, and his rapid-fire speech was bitter as he sat at the soda fountain in the Karankawa Drugstore and cursed Gator Coach John Foote.

"The man's an absolute damned idiot," Mousey declared. "He needs to be fired as soon as the season is over. Why, Tramp Majors could take this team and turn it around in a week."

Duke Grant, in the years that passed after that victorious team of '57 graduated had miraculously become an all-state player and a master of motivation. He was also chairman of the local school board, on the board of directors at the bank, and dictator to the Karankawa Chamber of Commerce. His anger at Coach John Foote was depthless, and after the humiliating loss to arch rival White City, his ire chafed him like an unscratchable itch. He called Coach Foote to his home for a conference on the football fortunes of Karankawa City.

They drank whiskey together in the same opulence that had hosted the '57 victory party. And Duke, stifling his ire as best he could, put on his good-old-boy charm and talked about everything but football until he felt the coach was properly softened.

Coach Foote, despite Mousey's questioning his native intelligence, was not an idiot. He knew full well why Duke Grant wanted to talk to him, and he waited patiently for the hammer to fall. It was not long in coming, but Duke's timing was not all it should have been. Coach John Foote had swallowed enough alcohol to be beyond caring. He did not intend to put up with one ounce of Duke Grant's meddling.

"I saw that old truck you drove here," Duke said. "You oughta get you a Cadillac like mine, make an impression on the community."

John Foote stretched his lanky frame, tried to relax and settle himself deeper into an overstuffed chair. "On my salary?" he asked, smiling.

"It's all a matter of motivation," Duke set his glass down and leaned toward the coach with the utmost confidence in his subtlety. "Just like football is a matter of motivation."

"I guess you're gonna have to explain that. I'm not sure I understand."

"Well, hell," Duke's voice rose an octave, "it's simple enough. You gotta motivate them boys, Foote, like old Tramp Majors done in '57. It don't make no difference whether it's football or bidness; motivation's the thing."

Coach Foote nodded and grinned. "Tramp Majors is coaching the Chargers right now, Mr. Grant, and I believe if you'll ask him, he'll tell you the professional football draft might come before motivation. Otherwise old Tramp and them would just play with whoever showed up—whether they weighed in at 300 or 150—and then motivate the hell out of 'em."

Duke Grant's face reddened. "That's what's wrong with all you damned school teachers . . . you too dumb to understand bidness. I'll bet my damned house that old Tramp could motivate these Gators!"

John Foote stood and poured himself another drink. "Well, if I understand your argument, you're sayin' Tramp Majors could take the Karankawa City Gators, motivate 'em enough, and then beat the Chargers. Is that right?"

"Damned right!" Duke retorted. "I *know* about motivation, Foote, how you think I ever got all this stuff I own?" Duke spread his arms to indicate the Grant empire.

"You inherited most of it," Coach Foote smiled evilly, "and you stole part of it, and the rest you kissed somebody's ass to get. Motivation had nothing to do with it. But I'll tell you what, Grant. If you're such a motivational expert, you should be able to motivate yourself, so drop your ass into a four-point stance. We'll go head-to-head, me and you. And if you're the motivator you think you are, why you oughta be able to whip my ass. Now put up or shut up, you pus-gutted bastard."

Duke Grant stared speechless at Coach John Foote for a moment, then yelled, "I *hire* that kind of shit done, Coach!"

"Then you ain't got too damned much confidence in motivation, do you, Grant?" Coach John Foote walked out of Duke Grant's home, got in his old pickup, and laughed all the way to Karankawa City.

The school board refused to renew his contract at mid-term. He was the fifth head football coach Karankawa City had used up in eight years.

Red Carlson drove through the streets of Karankawa City on a Sunday afternoon in February and looked around him at the changes twenty years had brought. He had visited his home often during that time, but he was always surpsied by the alterations in what he youthfully assumed would be constant. Main Street was still familiar to him; he recognized Mel Teat's Barber Shop, Scotty's Longhorn Saloon, and Bo's Gulf Service. But Main Street, called "downtown" when he was in high school, was no longer the center of Karankawa City's business district.

Most of the small retail stores were now located on Karankawa Avenue, which ran the length of the town from east to west and connected the throughways on either side of the city. In his youth,

Red had known Karankawa Avenue as a dead-end street with an asphalt surface and little traffic. But now, as he drove down that street, he was amazed at the four concrete lanes and the heavy, Sunday afternoon traffic. And he was even more astounded that most of the cars were driven by teenagers who seemed to honk and wave beer cans at each other with complete indifference to passing Karankawa City Police vehicles.

In the twenty years since Red Carlson had graduated from Karankawa High, he had become a journeyman football coach. Now almost thirty-nine years of age, he had coached in several Texas high schools and two of the state's smaller universities; he was also married and the father of two children. Like most young men who grew up in small Texas towns, he remembered the wonderful times and warm-hearted people who had surrounded him with affection and respect during his high school career. He could not imagine a better place to coach than Karankawa City, and as he drove through the town he was overwhelmed with nostalgia and the mental images that old sights and smells triggered.

Simple sights brought forth intoxicating memories.

A wisteria vine next to his father's house, though barren of purple flowers in winter, fetched up pictures of Ginger Herman, thirteen years old in a white blouse and blue jeans beneath an April moon. She gave him his first kiss. He was a year older than Ginger, but in his memory it seemed the *world* was only fourteen the morning after Ginger Herman. He walked into that morning barefoot and smiling. Early morning shadows leaned long, stretched out, and angled from tall trees, squat bushes, and tiny blades of grass. Infant sunlight, captured and sentenced to brief imprisonment in dew droplets, clung golden—like sparkling bits of silver and gold that fashioned necklaces for wisteria petals, jewels for wisteria leaves, and diamond crowns for wild buttercups at the vine's base—while a lizard lay wet, green, and flat, staring lidless into Red Carlson's quiet miracle of the morning after Ginger Herman.

He smiled now, at the memory that wisteria vine prompted, and ruefully understood what he had failed to understand then . . . it could only happen once, there was only one Ginger Herman, only one first kiss.

He felt the same way about Karankawa High School; that it was well over, done, before he really got into it, before he recognized it for what it was. It hung musty in his mind like a half-sung song. He was sure he had left its nooks and corners half-explored, girls half-loved, lessons half-learned; and the ghost of his half-lived youth still roamed its halls.

He saw the Karankawa Board of Trustees' offer—following the orders of Duke Grant—of the head coaching job as a chance to relive some of that, and to repay part of what he felt he owed to Karankawa High. He loved the place, and there was conviction in his mind when he accepted their offer.

"Red on the head, like a dick on a dog!" Duke Grant boomed after the board meeting completed the hiring of Red Carlson as Head Coach and Athletic Director of the Karankawa High Gators. He clapped Red on the back with a beefy hand and congratulated his fellow board members for doing the right thing for Karankawa City. "*Now* we'll get this damned show on the road. The Gators been a doormat long enough . . . been whupped up on by Beaumont and Port Arthur till I could puke. Now we gonna see some action, by God!"

Outside the Karankawa School District Administration Building, Hardhat Hastings, Little Hardhat—now twenty-nine years old—Mousey Kendall, Frog Mason, and a few other Gator Boosters waited for the board's decision. Duke Grant stood on the concrete steps and announced it to the world, "We hired Red Carlson, folks. And we're lookin' forward to another championship like him and old Tramp won in '57. Gonna give old Red everything he wants, and we hope all you Gator Boosters will support him like we have."

The crowd at the foot of the steps applauded and cheered the board's decision. And when Red Carlson walked among them they gave him hearty handshakes; some smiled and greeted him with hugs, and Mousey Kendall embraced him with tears streaming down sallow cheeks. Karankawa City hailed its football messiah with perfect confidence in his ability. Frog Mason was alone in his skepticism. "Good luck, son," Frog rasped in his gravel voice. "You damned sure gonna need it."

The first thing Red Carlson did was call Coach John Foote.

He was not enthusiastic about Red Carlson's hometown. "They still waitin' for '57, Red," Coach Foote said, "and I don't believe it's ever gonna come around again. Don't misunderstand me now, I know you're a good football coach, but I'm afraid that ain't gonna be enough. You got too many things to contend with, not even counting that damned 'Booster Club,' as they call it. You got precious few blacks, and none of them played football while I was there. You got lots of would-be country club types who won't even consider playing football. You got Duke Grant, who thinks Knute Rockne halftime speeches will win for you. And you got Karankawa Avenue."

"What the hell does Karankawa Avenue have to do with it?" Red asked.

John Foote laughed bitterly, "Dope. Marijuana, cocaine, heroin, pills . . . whatever they want can be bought right there on Karankawa Avenue in your hometown, Red. I'm sorry, but I'm afraid it's true."

Red was silent for several seconds. "I don't believe that, Coach. How can that be true? Hell, this ain't Houston, Dallas, or Chicago; this is Karankawa City, Texas, man. These are country kids, not *country club* kids. These boys might be interested in girls and beer; so were we in '57. But that's normal. I don't believe we got dope addicts here."

"Then *don't* believe it, Red. But just remember that you ain't living in '57 any more than those so-called Gator Boosters. I ain't got no reason to lie to you, Red, and I'm tellin' you straight: it ain't the same sweet town you left at nineteen. You had better damned sure believe *that*."

But Red Carlson didn't believe John Foote. What he did believe in, like most athletes and coaches, was himself. He was cocky, and he honestly believed he could turn Karankawa City around. He told Frog Mason as much.

"I can outrun 'em and outfight 'em, Frog," Red said with confidence, as he and the old cowboy sat in deep grass beside a windmill on Frog's ranch and drank beer on a Saturday afternoon in May. "I'll do whatever is necessary to win."

Frog nodded and swallowed a half-can of beer before he spoke. "You a good boy, Red, you always was. And you're a fighter. But you better remember that you ain't got no eligibility left; they ain't gonna let you suit up and play no more. You gonna have to stand on the sideline and watch, just like me."

Red Carlson watched water pour from the windmill into the stock pond as he thought about that. "But I'll make 'em *be* like me. I'll teach 'em to be good football players, and I'll teach 'em to be good citizens. Hell, I know they'll drink a little beer and screw around some, but there ain't much harm in that."

"Shit!" Frog growled. "You gonna have to grow up! This ain't the same world it used to be. Look at me. Do I look like a damned bull rider anymore? You reckon I could compete now? Sure, you can out-run 'em and outfight 'em, but that don't count no more. What you'll have to do, if you want to stay here, is *out-think* 'em. And you ain't got an even start for that—you can't even imagine the things they'll do to mess you up. They'll lay awake nights making up ways to keep you from winning football games."

"What the hell you mean, Frog? You tryin' to tell me this town don't want to win anymore?"

Frog threw a beer can into the bed of his pickup. "You goofier'n six road lizards, boy. Hell yes, they want to win alright, but they want to do it on *their* terms. I can see it's gonna take a while for you to understand that, and by the time you do it'll probably be too late."

Coach Red Carlson didn't believe Frog Mason either.

During March, April, and May of Red Carlson's first year as head coach, there was little he could do but plan and oversee the weight-lifting and running of his prospective football players. He was not allowed, in Texas class 3A football, to have spring training, and he wasn't used to that. He didn't regard player conditioning as a waste of time, but he would have felt better had they been able to put on pads and hit each other. He nervously awaited the coming of August, when he could get some idea of what his players could do. Time dragged, as it always had done for Red Carlson between foot-ball seasons.

Old coaching friends came by to see him, watched his charges go through their off-season conditioning paces, and left shaking their heads sadly.

"I just came from watching White City work out," an assistant coach from Texas State University jokingly told him, "and there ain't but two differences between ya'll and them; they're big and fast and ya'll are little and slow. Jesus! These damned kids are wormy lookin'."

Red Carlson grinned and nodded. He was alarmed at the lack of team speed and size in Karankawa City, but he was sure he could overcome that with enthusiasm and desire. He intended his team to play with a fanaticism seldom seen in the annals of Texas high school football.

It didn't work out that way. He won the first game by one point, but he was far from satisfied with the team's effort. He made the practices harder; he demanded more effort from the players, his assistant coaches, and himself. He lost the second game by twenty points and hated himself.

Duke Grant came by after the loss and patted him on the back. "Don't worry about one loss, Red. Just try to motivate 'em more—get 'em fired up. You know how, like you and old Tramp done in '57."

The Gators lost the next four games, one to arch rival White City by almost forty points, and the Gator Boosters began to grumble.

Hardhat Hastings threw a fit when he got home from work on the Monday after the loss to the White City Tigers. "Somebody painted a picture of a damned tiger sittin' on top of an alligator on the side of one of our chemical tanks at Tex-Eco-Safe," Hardhat told Little Hardhat, who was still living with his parents at age twenty-nine. "Looks like we mighta hired another damned loser."

Little Hardhat's eyes were shining with the light of good Colombian pot as he grinned at his father, sipped whiskey from a shot glass, and watched cartoons on television. "Wish we could get old Tramp Majors back, he's prob'ly the only one alive can coach these damned Gators right."

Tramp Majors, even as Little Hardhat spoke, was coaching in the National Football League and enjoying a six-figure salary. But a surprising number of Gator Boosters were certain he would someday return and deliver them from defeat and the mocking jeers of victorious White Citians.

"I believe you may be right, son," Hardhat Hastings told the light of his life. "You been here long enough to know. Why hell, you was a Gator your-own-self."

Little Hardhat *had been* a Gator for a short period. But in 1963, when Karankawa City was still enjoying winning football seasons and Little Hardhat was a high school junior, he had been kicked off the team for not attending practice. Time after time Little Hard-hat had begged his mother to call the coach's office and report him ill. She did as Little Hardhat asked—even when he telephoned his illness to her then drove his car up and down Karankawa Avenue while his teammates practiced in Texas autumn heat. All that ended when an assistant coach's wife saw him driving and drinking a can of beer on Karankawa Avenue during football practice. And when the coach questioned Little Hardhat's mother about his whereabouts, she reaffirmed his illness.

She and her son were caught in a lie, and Hardhat Hastings never forgave the coach for catching them. He was glad when the man left Karankawa City for a better job, and afterwards he never trusted another Karankawa High coach.

Little Hardhat, however, was relieved. He didn't want to play football anyhow, and getting kicked off the team was an easy way out. That way he could blame the coach and be a hero to his non-participant friends who were just beginning to learn about the joys of marijuana on Karankawa Avenue.

And now, as Red Carlson labored through eighteen-hour days and seven-day weeks to make Karankawa City a winner, Little Hard-hat smoked dope, drank whiskey, watched cartoons on television, and prayed for the return of Tramp Majors. The elder Hastings went to work each morning, suffered the biting scorn of his White City co-workers at Tex-Eco-Safe, and truly began to hate Red Carlson. And Duke Grant, whose idea it had been to hire Red, was put in the position of backing up that recommendation or agreeing with Red's detractors. "All of you know it ain't easy for me to say I was wrong," he finally told the Karankawa Board of Trustees, "but I'm gonna have to say it—I was wrong about Red Carlson."

Everyone in Karankawa City, except Red and his coaches, heard of Duke's admission and admired him for it. They told each other what a big man it took to admit he was wrong. "Good old Duke," Mousey Kendall said to a group of Gator Boosters in his drug store, "that's just like him. When he makes a mistake he'll own up to it. And he damned sure made a mistake with Red Carlson."

The Karankawa City Gator Boosters nodded in agreement. And none of them, not even Mousey himself, remembered how Mousey had shed tears of joy at the hiring of Red Carlson, or how most of them had grasped Red's hand and congratulated him. And none of them remembered his performance as a player in that memorable '57 season; they were only interested in what Red had done for them *lately*.

The Gators ended the season with three wins and seven losses, and wherever two Gator Boosters met, the disaster was with them also. It was discussed in Mel Teat's Barber Shop, at Scotty's Longhorn Saloon, and Bo's Gulf Service on Main Street—Mousey Kendall ranted and raved at his drugstore counter, Duke Grant strode the sidewalks of the business district and repeatedly confessed his great mistake, and Gator Boosters everywhere wondered what could be done. For Red Carlson had a year left on his contract. To fire him meant paying him off, and thirty thousand dollars was more than the good citizens of Karankawa City were prepared to pay. Red and his family, they reasoned, were not worth the money—even if winning was.

Gator players were told by Gator Boosters, many of whom were player parents, that Red Carlson was suspect. Men who had taken jobs at Tex-Eco-Safe because going to college seemed like a lot of work with no pay—who had laughed at Red Carlson while he suffered through his college years broke and without transportation—were, nevertheless, frustrated football coaches. They were the coaches of local little league football teams. They carried playbooks larger than those in the NFL, wore "coaching" shorts about town, called each other "Coach" as often as possible, and assured all who listened that they, if only given the opportunity, could do a much better job than Red Carlson. Little Hardhat Hastings was foremost among them.

Hardhat Hastings, true to his Buzzard Roost Prairie rearing, had taught Little Hardhat bigotry, and the younger Hastings proved to be an apt learner. In the eyes of teenaged Gator football players, Little Hardhat was a grown man and a football coach himself. He talked to Gator players at every opportunity. "There just ain't no way them damned fools can beat ya'll," Little Hardhat told his young listeners. "It's your sorry coach that's the problem. Your coach ain't wuth a shit."

Perhaps, if the players hadn't heard their parents say the same thing, they wouldn't have believed Little Hardhat. But wherever they went the message was the same: Red Carlson was not a good football coach. And they came to believe it was the truth.

Karankawa Avenue traffic became heavier after football season. As soon as school ended each weekday, the pizza salons, hamburger palaces, and fried chicken emporiums on every Karankawa Avenue corner prospered. Trans-Am sportcars, pickup trucks, and family cars driven by semi-affluent Karankawa City teens flooded parking lots. Hard rock music blared from car radios, and sinister-looking vans cruised up and down Karankawa Avenue selling whatever turned the kids on. The traffic increased on weekends, and by Sunday afternoon the street was avoided by adults. The parents of those Karankawa High students who cruised "the Drag," as they called it, drove blocks out of their way to keep from crossing Karankawa Avenue.

Little Hardhat Hastings drove a van. He could be found cruising the Drag every Sunday afternoon, and the kids loved him. He commiserated with their complaints about parents, teachers, and Red Carlson, and he sold them their favorite narcotic. Little Hardhat could be counted on, they told each other, to provide any escape from reality that they needed, and he amused Karankawa High athletes with stories of his football prowess, his dope-selling "scores," and the whores he could provide them. Little Hardhat was much more popular in Karankawa City than Red Carlson.

Red Carlson had been in Karankawa City for less than a year when Karankawa Avenue made *News Minute* magazine. The magazine, a chronicler of happenings across the nation, featured an article which explored similar problems that teen drags in five other states had caused business and commerce. In every other instance city police had put a stop to the problem; only in Karankawa City had merchants complained when the police tried to stop the bumper-to-bumper traffic on Karankawa Avenue. "The afternoon and weekend traffic is good for bidness," Karankawa merchants told the city council, Duke Grant, and the chamber of commerce, "and whatever is good for bidness is good for Karankawa City."

Mousey Kendall and Hardhat Hastings agreed with the council

decision to divert police attention elsewhere. "Leave the kids alone," the council ordered, "they ain't hurtin' nothing and we need the bidness. Bidness is the lifeblood of this whole country."

Little Hardhat, of course, was elated because stopping teen traffic might have interfered with his business.

"Hah," Frog Mason told Red Carlson as they doctored a sick cow on his ranch in December, "it don't make no difference nohow. The only way them Karankawa poleece could catch a damned crim'nal is if he come into Mousey's drugstore and *surrendered* while they drankin' coffee. 'Cause that's where they usually all at."

And winter and spring passed while Red Carlson waited for the next football season and a chance to redeem himself. He talked to every coach he respected, called Tramp Majors and asked his advice, and demanded more work from his assistants. He worked his players harder during the off-season and many of them got tired of the daily grind—weightlifting and running exacted its toll—and he lost seventeen players, ten of whom became regular customers of Little Hardhat. And for every player that quit, Red Carlson made at least two implacable enemies. The players' parents became even more convinced that "there's a real problem up at that high school," and in their minds the Red Carlson taint spread to the classroom and administration. The quitters' parents complained to other parents, and by the time the season started, the Gator Booster Club had swelled by ninety percent with haters of Red Carlson.

After school started that September, Red walked the halls and talked to teachers, some of whom had taught him at Karankawa High. He solicited the help of administrators, counselors, and maintenance personnel. "Help me get this team on the right track," he begged.

He was met with uneasiness among the faculty. There was anxiety in the administrators—on several occasions he thought they looked around them furtively as they talked to him, as if they were afraid someone might see them in his presence. A week of trying sent him to Frog Mason.

"It's like I have a damned *disease*," he told Frog, "like I'm contagious or something. What the hell's the matter with these people?"

"You a loser, as far as they concerned," Frog answered slowly. "They don't want to be connected to that, and they don't want to get too close to you if there's a chanc't you might get fired. Now you wait, if you figger some way to win, why they'll be tickled to talk to you. You'll have more damned friends than you can shake a stick at."

The Gators had lost five and won one, there were four games left on the schedule, and the auditorium was full when Red Carlson met with angry Gator Boosters to show them the film of the most recent loss.

Red was sick and confused. The powerful frame that had demolished running backs and enemy linemen had lost twenty pounds. His cocksure attitude had been replaced by bitterness, and the warm husband and father was changed into a cold and indifferent stranger. Red's wife had even begun to doubt him, "I wish you were different," she said one night when he was more despondent than usual.

"Why is it," a female Gator Booster asked when Red finished showing the film, "that other teams have boys who can run fast? Why don't we have boys that can run fast?"

Red saw it as another indictment of his coaching, the Gator Booster blaming him for Karankawa City's lack of speed. "Because," Red told the mother of a Gator football player, "boys in other towns have fast mamas and daddies. And that's the same reason you don't see many jackasses in the Kentucky Derby."

It was the ungilded truth, but unpalatable to the packed auditorium. And as Red was later told in his evaluation conference, by an assistant superintendent who lisped, had a limp wrist, and didn't know a cornerback from a jockstrap, "It's just bad public relations."

"The truth always is," Red answered.

Red Carlson's team lost three of the next four games, and he was non-renewed at mid-term. He lost no time moving his family out of Karankawa City.

Duke Grant, during the two years Red Carlson was struggling to win football games, had worked long and hard to procure a low-interest government loan for a housing project on the outskirts of Karankawa City. He explained how the new apartment complex would be "good for bidness," and he got the full cooperation of all the prominent merchants in town. He left out some details in his many presentations to the city council, but the council trusted Duke's judgement and didn't question him extensively.

"Good old Duke," Mousey Kendall told all Gator Boosters who appeared in his drugstore, "I just don't know what we would do without him."

And Hardhat Hastings, who wasn't a businessman but claimed to be interested in anything that might help Karankawa City prosper, was effusive in his praise for Duke and his entrepreneuring nature. "Free enterprise," he told Little Hardhat, "that's the American way. Bidness and industry . . . people like Duke make this country what it is. We'll all be free as long as we got folks like Duke Grant. It's men like him that'll keep the undesirables and guviment from taking over this country."

Little Hardhat said he agreed with the free enterprise and goverment part.

Construction of the apartment complex began at about the time Red Carlson left, and it took two years to complete. During those two football seasons the Gators continued to suffer humiliating losses, while the *Karankawa County News* pointed out how good the building was for the local economy, and all Karankawans engaged in the construction business profited. And at a ribbon-cutting ceremony on the day the complex—called Grant's Manor—opened for business, Duke Grant mouthed important platitudes about the positive impact it would have on the local economy. It was a big event in Karankawa County, and Mousey Kendall stood next to Hardhat Hastings and shed tears as both applauded Duke's speech. "The best thing about this," Hardhat told Mousey, "is that old Duke did it on guviment money. It ain't cost us nothin', and that's what free enterprise is all about."

Mousey Kendall agreed.

Karankawans made it a point to drive past Grant's Manor whenever they could, and they were impressed with its concrete, steel, and glass eminence. They spoke to relatives in other parts of Texas and explained how Karankawa City had begun to grow and take its rightful place beside Beaumont and Port Arthur. And Duke Grant accepted their praise with thinly veiled hubris. "It was the logical thing to do," Duke told his admirers. "We're halfway between Houston and Baton Rouge, we can't help but grow."

Grant's Manor had been in operation less than three months when the black families began to move in.

Karankawans had long ago accepted the presence of the few black families – descended from servants and ranch hands who had come in the late nineteenth century – living in pieced-together homes near the Kolander pasture. Working as maids or doing yard work for the Karankawa elite, these people were seen as necessary in the scheme of things in Karankawa City. "Them's *our* niggers," Karankawans told outsiders, "and they stay in their place. We don't never have no problem with them."

But the arrival of strange blacks created a scandal in Karankawa City, and Hardhat Hastings was beside himself with anger. "Blood's gonna run knee-deep to a tall horse!" Hardhat yelled at Gator Boosters and anyone else who would listen. "I ought to have knowed that guviment money would bring them here."

"It was Duke Grant who got that money, Hardhat," Frog Mason growled. "What you gonna do about him? Maybe we oughta go right on out there to his ranch and *lynch* him, since you so damned worried about his tenants. Hell, it's his fault they're here and I want a ringside seat to watch you chew his ass out about it."

"Aw hell, Frog," Hardhat said, "old Duke didn't have no idear who was gonna move in out there. Else he wouldn't have *touched* none of that guviment money."

"Well good," Frog said, "then put on your damned bedsheet and go to Grant's Manor and burn a cross or somethin'. Run all them black folks off so good old Duke loses his ass and all its fixtures because he ain't got no renters. He'll love that."

Hardhat Hastings didn't like it, but there was nothing he and the local KKK could do but proclaim their hatred for the black families at Grant's Manor. Even their bigotry wasn't enough to spur them into facing Duke Grant and his influence.

The lower middle-class black families stayed, almost a hundred of them, and the problems they had were generally confined to minor skirmishes at Karankawa High School, lack of acceptance into white society, and the inescapeable acts of prejudice they experienced everywhere. Their children rode yellow school buses to and from school each day, studied their lessons, and kept to themselves. Black teenagers couldn't afford automobiles, so they didn't drive up and down the Drag and participate in its drug culture. Besides, they were quite sure they wouldn't have been accepted there anyway. And their parents, who had leaped at the chance to escape the atmosphere of drugs and alcohol in the ghettos where they had lived before, kept those dangers to a minimum in Grant's Manor.

But the black teenagers *did* participate in sports, and the Gator football team began to improve. In 1980, the Gators won six and lost four. And in the spring of 1981, as both boys and girls practiced their track skills at Gator Stadium, a black girl, Shureka Matthews, outran every white male athlete in Karankawa City.

Rodney Randall, the second coach hired in the four years since Red Carlson's departure, became the darling of the Karankawa Gator Boosters. "Damn," Hardhat Hastings told his friends, "we finally got us a good football coach."

Duke Grant could not have agreed more. "Knows somethin' about motivation," Duke said, "just like I been sayin' for years—motivation wins."

Mousey Kendall was so overcome that he cried copious tears, and in 1986, when War Hoss Kelly and his team won the state championship, Mousey fainted dead away and wet his pants.

The Karankawa High School cafeteria couldn't have held one more person at the football banquet honoring the 1986 Gator team. CLASS 3A STATE CHAMPS, 1986, proclaimed the banner stretched behind Tramp Majors as he addressed the happy Gator Boosters arrayed before him in their Sunday best.

Tramp was retired from football coaching and he was enjoying a life of beer, dominoes, and quarterhorses. As he came to the end of his talk, which had mainly praised the efforts of players and coaches, he looked down at the podium and read the yellowed newspaper clipping there: "We win . . . They lose . . ." the clipping said.

He looked out over the young faces of the players, most of whom were black, and he said in closing, "As I stand here looking at the

118

'86 champions of Texas, I am reminded of what Duke Grant and the Gator Boosters told me about another championship team in 1957. 'Blood will tell,' they said. 'Blood will tell.' And I believe they were right."

And Tramp Majors sat down amid thunderous applause.

The Click

A year before the click, while driving through Deep East Texas one morning, watching as dawn slanted into a wooded hollow and was captured by a fog-mist that glowed — like a goblet whose amber radiance had overflowed its rim and poured onto the forest floor — Owen Cabot saw three deer standing hip deep in golden light. Wraith-like, stone still, and staring at him with ears pointed upward toward damp pine needles, they hovered between flight and curiosity. Delicate, perfectly formed creatures that belonged exactly where they stood, that lived in the forest as only they knew how to live, that were planted there the same way its trees were planted, Owen thought.

And he was filled with a great longing to go home.

It was a four-lane highway where Owen saw the deer, and he drove over it twice a day. It runs from Beaumont through East Texas, and it's often called the Eastex Freeway by those who make radio and television commercials for businesses on either side of it. In Beaumont, a large shopping mall fronts on it, just before it crosses the LNVA Canal and becomes a country highway instead of a city freeway. The area between the mall and the Big Thicket area of Deep East Texas is caught up in a decision-making process, trying to decide whether it will remain country or become part of the city.

Owen knew the city would win, because cities always do.

He looked at the concrete wall daily. It was built down the center of the highway and topped by a mesh-wire fence, designed, Owen figured, to keep drivers from crossing the median and killing each other. Owen had noticed how such walls had become common of late and very effectively blocked a driver's view of the other side. The wall channeled his vision straight ahead — and he smiled wryly, as he thought how often his vision was required to be channeled straight ahead.

A week before the click, on the afternoon he saw the armadillo, he was driving south down the same highway, toward Beaumont, on a warm, spring day in May. It was during that rushed, driving-home-from-work period, and the traffic was furious. Huge diesel trucks roared past him, and rabid, tired workers vied with them for driving space.

He had no idea how far armadillos could see, or how well they could hear, but he knew they were quiet, innocuous creatures—shy and unusually timid. He knew they never bothered anyone, and if caught they rolled up in a tight ball and tried to disappear; like an ostrich thinks it does when it sticks its head in the sand.

He thought he probably saw the armadillo before anyone else did; he drove as slowly as the traffic permitted, and watched closely. He saw the animal dart into the highway, cross the first lane, dodge a pickup truck in the second lane, and make it to the concrete wall. Perhaps, Owen thought, the armadillo couldn't see the wall from his side of the highway, or maybe he didn't look—his errand might have been too important to stop him. But the concrete wall stopped him.

And Owen Cabot began thinking about walls.

The wall, as Owen watched the little armadillo race down it—heading south with the flow of traffic, frantically searching for a way through—suddenly loomed taller and broader in his mind. It became the Berlin Wall, the wire fence between Texas and Mexico; it became the fences around Auschwitz, Buchenwald, and every wall erected in human history to keep people in, or out. And, in Owen's mind, it symbolized all those invisible walls society erects in people's minds, beyond which thought and compassion are not to go.

The armadillo didn't make his second trip across the highway; an eighteen wheeler got him just as he started to go home.

But Owen knew it wasn't just the truck that killed him. It was his trying to go home, and that damned concrete wall . . . waiting.

Owen didn't see the deer again, and he knew he would never see them. He knew they had slipped away through the golden mist, quietly, and gone deeper into the Big Thicket where there weren't any concrete walls yet . . . trying to go home.

Two days before the click, Owen looked at his Karankawa County ranch and felt like a part of it.

If he had been a Longhorn bull, he thought, or a stud horse instead of a man, and if some ancient Mexican vaquero had looked upon the ranch through sad, wisdom-filled eyes, touched its deep grass with big, scarred, dark old Mexican-vaquero hands, lifted its heavy loam and sniffed at it, tasted it, and looked inside Owen Cabot until he perceived the raw ends of the feelings there, then that old Mexican vaquero would have known what to call it. He would have looked into the raw feelings, nodded a sombreroed head, and murmured softly, "Sí, es tu querencia."

Then the old Mexican vaquero would have mounted a skinny, black horse and ridden away. And he would have understood, perfectly, the pain of it, because he would have known the old stories.

He would have known how old bulls and horses can have a particular spot they love, a place that somehow fits them, where they stand for hours, days, years, a lifetime—maybe in the shade of a particular tree—and feel comfortable and at peace with the world. He would have heard about Longhorn lead steers which, after several trips from Texas to Kansas, were sometimes lost, stolen, or sold hundreds of miles from home, only to reappear months later; hungry, footsore, and with ribs showing through ragged, roan hides, dozing under the same tree. And he would have sensed why the Mexicans, with deep understanding, feeling an affinity and a kinship with the animal, gave such places a name—*querencia*, a heart's love, a place of belonging, the country of one's blood.

No one had asked, and if they had he would have told them how it wasn't a job for a grown man anyway. He would have said he had decided that the morning one of his teachers (he was a principal) refused to clean up the puke in the school cafeteria. He would have told how there was a sort of click in his mind when he used a second sight that allowed him to watch himself in action. He would have described himself watching himself, the irate teacher, and the small boy beside her with half-dried vomit on his clothes in the tiny office. He would have explained how the office was painted a sickly green that had made him nauseated for five years, how the dry vomit smelled, how the plaster was cracked on the ceiling, and how the telephone on his cluttered desk was a bright orange color. He had never seen an orange telephone before, and every day he wondered why anyone would put an orange telephone in a sick-green office.

It was the sick-green walls, the orange telephone, the vomit on the boy's shirt, and the irate teacher that overwhelmed him, finally, and caused the click.

"Who's gonna clean up the puke?" the teacher asked. She rested clenched fists on her hips and talked through clenched teeth and tight lips with just the hint of a quiver at their corners.

He watched himself lean back in his principal's chair—carefully, because it was on rollers, and one of them often came loose when he leaned too far back, and deposited him on the floor, which he found undignified—as he asked softly, "To which particular puke do you refer?"

As he asked the question, he saw himself studying the tight lips of the teacher, and he realized she was tight-lipped whether she was angry or not. And he wondered if she was from Oklahoma. For he had long ago decided Oklahoma produced a lot of tight-lipped people who spoke through clenched teeth, whether they were mad or not.

"Or maybe West Texas," he murmured absently, before the teacher had a chance to explain what specific puke she was talking about.

The tight-lipped teacher frowned and shook her head. She was confused. "What does West Texas have to do with it?"

He wanted to explain the click in his brain, how he was watching himself watch himself, and how many tight-lipped, clenched-teeth people came from Oklahoma and West Texas. But he didn't. It would only have confused her further.

"Forget West Texas," he watched himself say, "and just tell me what the hell you're talkin' about." And as he saw himself ask the question, he wondered what the woman from the Texas Education Agency would think if she heard him curse in front of a teacher and a small boy. And he wondered what the woman from the Agency had thought of him anyway, after she left at the end of her visitation to evaluate him and his school two months ago.

"Tell me," she had asked him before her visitation began (they were sitting in his tiny office with the sick-green walls and the

orange telephone), "what you see as your main role as an elementary principal."

When the Agency woman asked the question, his mind immediately searched through itself until it came upon a voluminous com-
munique from the Agency which explained the role of the principal
in tedious detail. But he couldn't remember the details, all he could
remember was that the Agency had misspelled role: R-O-L-L. So he
gave the Agency woman a bad answer. "My main function is to protect the teachers from the community."

She gave him a blank stare for a good while, he thought. Then
she started scribbling in her notebook. He was quite sure she was
giving him a big, fat minus on that answer. And he remembered,
as he watched himself ask the question of the tight-lipped, clenched-
teeth teacher, how he hadn't cared in the least *what* the Agency
woman wrote in her little notebook. And he remembered wondering whether she misspelled role too, when she wrote down her question and his honest answer.

The Agency woman hadn't met Mr. Yary, who owned the only
grocery store in town, seven rent houses, and was president of the
school board. If she had, then she might have known how honest
his answer was. Mr. Yary smiled a lot and let poor people charge
groceries, and he rented his houses to people on welfare — white people, because they were more dependable with their welfare checks
every month — and every month those people signed their checks
over to Mr. Yary. And at the school board's private meetings, Mr.
Yary bemoaned the government giving away the country to "lazy
bastards who won't work."

Mr. Yary was just the *main* person the Agency woman hadn't
met. She also hadn't met the textbook censors, nor the religious
diehards who not only wanted prayer in school but wanted to *lead*
the prayers, and she hadn't met the parents who didn't want their
children sitting next to "niggers." And the Agency woman hadn't
met those Deep East Texans who put bumper stickers on their beat-
up trucks that said, "This vehicle protected by Smith & Wesson,"
and carried axes and chainsaws on the seat beside them. (He saw
himself wondering what on earth they needed to protect those decrepit trucks from.)

And the Agency woman hadn't met Big Bertha, who wanted to

beat up a teacher once a month. And those were just a few of the people the Agency woman hadn't met. He figured those people might have had some bearing on the click in his head too.

"I don't believe it's part of my duties as a teacher," said the tight-lipped teacher, "to clean up puke in the school cafeteria. But the women who work in the cafeteria refuse to clean it up. And I'm here to tell you it's not in my job description."

"Send the boy on back to the classroom," he told the tight-lipped teacher, "you don't need him any longer. I'm thoroughly convinced he did, indeed, puke. Let him go wash his face."

He watched himself question his humanitarianism toward the child. Because he wasn't entirely sure that sending the boy away was anything more than wanting to be rid of the smell of vomit. And he watched himself wondering if this was a job for a full-grown man.

"Those cafeteria people are gettin' so uppity . . ." And he watched himself turn off the tight-lipped teacher's voice while he remembered how the school dietician had asked the school board not to let hungry kids charge lunches any more. He remembered how Mr. Yary had jumped on the idea, agreeing instantly, and complaining the school cafeteria wasn't making any money. He remembered telling Mr. Yary and the other board members, "I didn't know a school cafeteria was supposed to make money." And he remembered how they had stared him down without answering.

He had solved that problem by buying a huge jar of peanut butter, some grape jelly and apple butter, and a couple of loaves of bread. He placed them on a table at the school entrance, and behind them he put a sign that said, FOR KIDS WHO CAN'T AFFORD LUNCHES IN THIS SCHOOL'S CAFETERIA — COMPLIMENTS OF THE FACULTY.

Nobody had said a word to him, but the new no-charge policy was changed at the next board meeting. And Mr. Yary quit smiling at him.

"Ask the janitor if he would mind cleaning up the puke in the cafeteria," he saw himself say to the tight-lipped teacher. "It's not his job either, but ask him if he'll do it as a favor to me."

Thirty mintues later, he watched himself staring at a janitor who was so mad that every muscle in his body was quivering. He watched himself listen as the janitor raved about having to clean up puke in the cafeteria. He watched himself tell the janitor, "I know it's bad duty, but if you think you're gonna come in here and chew my ass out about it, you're full of shit." And he knew it was a bad answer, but he attributed it to the click.

That afternoon, at four o'clock, he watched himself load all his personal things in a box; a picture of his family, a pen and pencil set, a western painting the faculty had given him, and a few books. He saw himself load them in his old truck and begin the sixty-mile drive southward to his Karankawa County ranch.

And as he drove toward home he saw himself singing a Mac Davis song, to which he substituted words without conscious effort.

"Happiness is Deep East Texas in the rearview mirror . . ."

126

About Jimmy Gene

I need to straighten up all those ugly Karankawa County stories about Jimmy Gene.

This is the way it really was:

In the long autumn afternoons of our tenth year, we walked the few blocks from Karankawa Elementary to the high school every day. We passed the "haunted house" on the corner of Sycamore and Fifth slowly, looking over the peeling picket fence, through breaks in the weeds, tall grass, and profusion of grape vines that hung from the giant oaks, looking into the shrouded windows on the second floor for the least sign of a ghost.

We never say one.

But one day Jimmy Gene and I crawled up close enough to the back door—it was nearer to the road behind the house and made it easier to run than if we snooped in front—to see an old woman with long, gray hair shuffling around the kitchen. We could see her easily through the screen door and we agreed she wasn't a ghost. But that didn't matter, it was deliciously scary, enough to make us crawl through the tall weeds and watch through the screen.

Besides, we both knew if we wanted to pretend the old woman was a ghost she would instantly become one.

After that first time, in September, we made it a point to sneak up on the haunted house every day. It was our first stop on the way to the high school.

Our second stop, not counting the times we kneeled in the dusty road to pet dogs, examine bugs, or touch touch-me-nots and watch them fold tiny leaves like fingers clasping together in prayer, was the drugstore soda fountain. The Karankawa Drugstore was owned by Mousey Kendall, who was both pharmacist and soda jerk, and it smelled of drugs, coffee, and the cigar smoke from the old men who gathered there to talk to Mousey about the Karankawa Gator football team.

Most days Jimmy Gene and I could scrape up enough pennies between us to make a nickel, which was the price of a fountain coke. Then we got two straws and shared it. When we didn't have enough money, we knew how to get a coke anyway. All we had to do was empty the pockets of our overalls on the counter and look sadly at each other. Frog Mason would always give us a nickel when we did that.

Our last stop was Karankawa High School, and we usually got there in time to see the Karankawa Gator football team take calisthenics. Jimmy Gene and I were allowed to borrow an old football and throw passes to each other. I never thought about it then, back in 1944, because we had grown up next door to each other and played together all our lives, but Jimmy Gene threw great passes for a girl.

I never considered asking her if she wanted to do anything besides watch the Gators practice after school. If she ever wanted to do something else, she never mentioned it. She seemed as happy throwing, catching, and kicking as I was, and while we walked home in near darkness, we usually talked about my future as a Karankawa Gator football player. I can't remember us ever discussing her future.

Most Friday nights in the fall, Jimmy Gene and I sat together in Gator Stadium and shared warm bags of roasted peanuts and watched the Gators. Our fathers were good friends and neighbors, and they took us with them to watch the road games too. All that was in the fall, of course.

In winter, unless the weather was too cold—which usually wasn't the case in Karankawa County—Jimmy Gene and I walked to the high school and watched Gator basketball practice. And during their breaks, we could dribble and shoot in Gator Gymnasium.

In spring, it was baseball and track, and Jimmy Gene and I were there almost every day. We were inseparable, except when we parted each evening to go home.

When school was out for the summer we played with the other neighborhood kids—baseball mostly, and kick-the-can—and occasionally we slipped off and went swimming together. She sort of cramped the style of my male friends who wanted to swim naked in the rice canals, but they came to tolerate her after I fought two of them about it. Sometimes she acted like a girl, and whenever they made her cry I fought with them.

So that's the way it was with me and Jimmy Gene, until we both turned thirteen and I started playing junior high football, and she became a cheerleader for the Junior Gators. But even then we were together at the games, and she always had a special smile for me when I trotted off the field with the badges of honor—dirt, blood, and sweat—on my face. And after every game she would run up and hug me whether we won or lost. Then, yeah, she started to look different, and my feelings about her changed.

Back when we stalked the haunted house she was straight as a stick and her strawberry blonde hair wasn't much longer than mine. But by the time she became a cheerleader she began to change. She had that honey-cream, smooth skin all the way from her toes to where it disappeared inside her cheerleader shorts and reappeared in the line of her graceful neck. The strawberry blonde hair hung in billows about her face and bounced when she walked. The plethora of freckles on her face vanished, except for seven (I counted) which were perfectly arranged across her nose like tiny flakes of gold. Her eyes, green-flecked-with-gold, lost that shiny-bright little-girl mirthfulness and turned into twin green mysteries.

And she began to make my groin ache.

See, football isn't a game in Karankawa County, Texas. It's a religion, and it's practiced every day—365 days a year—by the faithful. Friday nights are reserved for communion, and thousands turn out to watch and partake of blood sacrifices made by adolescent boys.

The nearest thing to Karankawa County football is the code of Japanese samurai, *bushido*, "the way of the warrior," and all it entails: trial by combat, honor, disgrace, and even a kind of social hara-kiri, for those who fail, is expected of Karankawa County players and coaches.

Jimmy Gene understood all that as well as I did. How could she not have? She and I heard it together in the Karankawa Drugstore as we sipped a Coke through straws and listened to Hardhat Hastings

and Mousey Kendall extol the prowess of some players, then bitterly curse those who didn't measure up to their expectations. We
heard it from our fathers as we sat in the darkened back seat of a
car and traveled to Gator games all over Southeast Texas. We heard
it at Gator practices, from coaches whose very lives depended on
how well they taught the way of the warrior. We intuited it as we
walked home from Gator practices as children, unescorted and un-
reprimanded for detouring by the high school and arriving home
in darkness. We both *knew* our parents felt it was a wholesome way
for us to spend long autumn afternoons.

She understood it alright. How could she not have, when she
knew her father had picked the name, Jimmy Gene, for a son and
refused to change it when he had a daughter instead?

We were friends until we were fifteen. Our friendship ended when
we became lovers.

*(Oh God, Jimmy Gene, Jimmy Gene! Why did we do it? Why couldn't
we stay ten years old in bib overalls, drinking Coke through two straws
in the Karankawa Drugstore forever?)*

We were in high school then, sophomores in 1949, and I was playing on the big Gator team.

"No more of that junior high shit *now*, boy!" Coach Noonan
screamed at me the first day of practice. "If you want something soft,
go to the shithouse and get you a double handful!"

The senior players tried their best to kill me. I trudged home
dead tired every day, with Jimmy Gene beside me (she always waited
for me after cheerleader practice) and books under my arm; my al-
gebra teacher was almost as serious as my football coach. And I
hurt. I hurt all over, and I often had scratches and cuts on my face.

"Poor, sweet baby," Jimmy Gene traced the cuts with soft, tapered
fingers and whispered to me. "Poor, sweet boy." And she looked at
me through those green-gold mysteries with softness.

God, how I loved Jimmy Gene!

But the seniors couldn't kill me. I got stronger, tougher, and by
the middle of the season I was giving as good as I took. I gained
weight, put on twenty pounds of solid muscle, my shoulders and
chest thickened. I began to make it through practice without suf-
fering total exhaustion . . . I was merely tired. I no longer hurt, and

one day I even told Jimmy Gene I would race her home after practice, like we used to do.

She shook her head and looked at me as though seeing me for the first time. "No. I can't stay up with you anymore."

I knew it was true. "Okay, then we'll walk," I grinned at Jimmy Gene.

I was a starter at tight end for the last two ball games, and Jimmy Gene was ecstatic.

"So now you're a big shot," she smiled at me one day during the last week of football practice. "A Gator starter, for goodness' sake."

We were walking home together again. I kicked at a can on the roadside with a little hop-step-kick motion, like I was trying for an extra point.

"Yep," I smiled at her. "Startin' for the Gators."

"Prob'ly get a letter jacket."

"Prob'ly," I nodded.

"Look at me." It was dusky-dark, November, and the days were short. The air blew in cool, damp, and heavy from the Gulf; there was a hint of winter in it and it smelled of burning leaves. Jimmy Gene stepped in front of me and put her hands on my shoulders. "Look at me," she said again.

"I'm lookin', Jimmy Gene," I said. "I'm lookin'."

"Well, goddammit, what do you see?"

"I see you. What else?"

"I'm a girl, you dumb football player. A *girl!* I'm not your little friend who sneaks up on haunted houses anymore. I'm a grown-up girl!"

"I know that, Jimmy Gene. Shit, I ain't blind."

"The hell you're not. You don't see me the way I am. You don't see me the way you see that prissy snot, Sue Ann Blair! I've seen the way you look at her in our English class!"

"Jesus, Jimmy Gene . . ." I felt confused, disoriented.

"Kiss me!"

I stared a good ten seconds before I dropped my books on the road.

Then I kissed Jimmy Gene.

Okay. I had been too busy playing football. I had been too busy learning the way of the warrior. I had learned to ignore the pain in my groin which presented itself often, when I was with Jimmy Gene. I had told myself to *reason* it all out. Jimmy Gene, I had reasoned, is the best friend I have in the entire world. If I make a pass at her, maybe she'll get offended, and then we can't be friends anymore, I reasoned.

The kiss blew all that to hell and gone. The kiss made me dizzy, and I squeezed her to me so hard it's a wonder she didn't break. The breeze blew a roaring in my ears.

I held her to me. "I love you, Jimmy Gene," I told her. "I've loved you all my life."

"Me too," she whispered against my neck. "And if you weren't such a big, dumb shit, we wouldn't have wasted all this time."

"You're right," I smiled down at her. "But we'll make up for it." And I'm afraid we did.

Our fathers, mine and Jimmy Gene's, had a combination duck hunting and fishing cabin on Brand's Bayou. They shared the cabin, shared expenses, and had often taken Jimmy Gene and me with them on their hunting and fishing trips. It was isolated and virtually all members of both families had keys. It was too convenient, and they trusted us. After all, we had been inseparable all our lives, so whenever we explained we were going fishing or hunting together, our parents were delighted.

"Nobody ever saw two kids who had more in common," our folks laughed to each other. And they didn't know how right they were.

It went on for two and a half years, and I'll never understand why Jimmy Gene didn't get pregnant. I even began to think I was sterile. Then, at other times, when her period was messed up and she was late, I would lie in my bed at night and pray to God.

"God," I begged the Almighty, time after time, "just let her be alright this once, and I promise I'll never do it again."

Then, the day after she finished her period, Jimmy Gene and I would take another fishing trip. We were insatiable.

By the time we were seventeen and seniors at Karankawa High, we had it down to a science. Load the truck with fishing or hunting gear, stop and buy beer (we were too young, but the grocers thought we were buying it for our folks), turn on the radio and listen to Hank Williams, go straight to the cabin without wetting a hook when we got there, do our number, clean up and be home by nine o'clock in the evening.

No muss, no fuss, no trouble. Not ever. Our parents thought we were paragons of virtue.

(Oh, Jimmy Gene, Jimmy Gene. Nobody ever loved you like I do. You're the best part of me and God knows I miss you.)

Then, in the middle of the spring semester of our last year at Karankawa High, I got a football scholarship to Texas State University. It was part of the code, part of the way of the warrior, part of the Southeast Texas *bushido*; nobody turned such a thing down. Nobody. To do so was to commit social hara-kiri—Karankawa County folks would look at you as if you were dead. And Jimmy Gene knew all that, I'll swear she did.

That was in 1952, and neither Jimmy Gene's parents nor mine could have afforded university fees for their children.

She looked at me from the bed in the cabin on Brand's Bayou, through those gold-green eyes with hurt in them. "So you're gonna go off and leave me then?"

We had been through it all several times before.

"Okay, Jimmy Gene, what do you want me to do?" I extended my arms and spread my fingers in a gesture of hopelessness.

"Stay," she said simply. "Just stay."

"I can't," I told her, "you *know* that. You know what people expect of me. You know what my parents—and yours—expect."

"Never mind them," she said softly. "What do *you* want?"

"I want you. I want Texas State University and football. I want it all."

She shook her head. "You can't have it all. You know I can't go with you. You can't have it all."

"Jesus!" I screamed. "I'm not goin' to Ethiopia, Jimmy Gene. I'll be less than six hours away."

"It might as well be the moon," she said. "I can't imagine life with you not in it. Not even for one semester."

I knew that part was true. I was having a problem with it too.

"Wait for me," I told her. "I'll be back."

She sat up on the edge of the bed and shook her lovely head. The strawberry blonde hair cascaded over her shoulders and fell about her naked breasts. "No, you won't ever come back, I just know it. Only a person who looks like you will return for brief visits . . . but it won't be *you* anymore. Not really *you*. It'll all be different and screwed up and never the same again. You're just too dumb to see it."

"I've got to go. I can't stay in Karankawa County forever, Jimmy Gene."

Then *go*, goddammit! Just go and see what happens, you dumb ass!" Tears ran down her cheeks and traced the contours of her breasts.

She called me "Dumb Ass" from that day on. We were almost eighteen when I left.

She didn't wait. When I returned at mid-term, she was dating Bubba McCord. I didn't stay long, never even talked to her. I moped around the house and went duck hunting with my dad, but the sight of the cabin on Brand's Bayou made my stomach hurt. I went back to the university the day after Christmas. "Need to get settled back in," I told my friends and parents.

And that's the way it was. She and Bubba got married in the spring, and I played football.

Five years after I graduated from the university, after I had started coaching at North Texas, I just happened upon Jimmy Gene at the cabin on Brand's Bayou. She was sitting beside the water with a cane pole and a can of worms, all alone, and she didn't know I was there.

I almost turned and walked away, but I didn't. "Perch fishing, I guess." I didn't know what else to say.

She turned her head quickly and looked at me. I saw the difference immediately. It was in those gold-green mysteries and the tiny lines that had formed at their corners. There was coldness in them, hardness.

"Well, what ya say, Dumb Ass?" she smiled. "I understand you're gettin' all that old football you can stand."

"So how's married life?" I asked.

She patted the grass beside her. "Sit down right here and I'll tell you all about it."

I sat.

"It's like this," she said. "He puts on a hardhat every morning and drives to the refinery with a lunch bucket in the seat beside him;

134

that's where he is right now. Inside the lunch bucket are two bologna sandwiches—no mustard, cut the onions—and an apple. He comes straight home from work, gets there at three-forty-two on the dot, takes off his hardhat, and picks up the *Port Arthur News*. Then he lies down on the couch. He reads the sports page first, then the comics. If there's a mention of your name, and there often is, he yells at me to come from the kitchen. 'Your old boyfriend's in the paper again,' he tells me. Sometime between his arrival and Alley Oop he starts to fart on the couch. If he feels a particularly strong one coming on, he calls me again. He wants to share his best farts with me, I suppose. Then I feed him some meatloaf, he turns on the teevee, and that's it."

"That's it?" I asked.

"Pretty much," she nodded and frowned at the cork bobbing on the brown water. "Except on weekends. That's when he washes his pickup and cleans his shotgun. And on Friday nights we go watch the Gators play and he screams at the coaches, players, and officials."

"Are you happy, Jimmy Gene?"

"Nah," she turned and looked me dead in the eyes. "I ain't been happy since the day you left, Dumb Ass. I told you how it would be."

"You hate me for that, Jimmy Gene? God, I hope you don't hate me."

Her eyes warmed up some then, and for a while they became deep green mysteries again. "No, I couldn't ever hate you. I love you, is what I do. Why don't we go up to the cabin and see if that old bed still works?"

So that's what we did.

Ten years later, in 1971, I became the head football coach at my old high school. And it was a disaster. We won eight games in two years, and the Karankawa County wolves commenced to howl at my door.

"They talkin' ugly about you at the old drugstore, Dumb Ass. Say you know about as much about football as they do brain surgery." I was meeting her at the cabin often, after football season.

"The only reason they ain't experts on brain surgery," I told Jimmy Gene, "is it's not on television."

Then something worse happened. Jimmy Gene's husband, old

Bubba McCord, ran for the school board, and his total platform was to get rid of me.

"Old Bubba can't abide a loser," she told me one day at the cabin. "He cusses you every chance he gets. Of course he's never considered that he's neither a winner *nor* a loser, since he ain't never tried nothin'. Then, he's also jealous of you, always has been."

"You think he knows, . . ." I started to ask.

"Nah. I never told him a damned thing about us, except that we grew up neighbors and had always been friends. No, he's not jealous of you because of me, he's jealous because of the football."

"That makes no sense, Jimmy Gene."

"Sure it does. You're the big, macho-stud football player old Bubba never could be. He hates you for that, and firing you will grease his ego a whole bunch. You got to remember that Bubba grew up in Karankawa County too. He never could go to the drugstore and hear those old codgers brag on him. No, every time he went they were talkin' about you and the Karankawa Gators. Now he's gonna get even."

In April of that year the town elected Bubba McCord to the school board. They fired me a year later, which I figure they would have done even without Bubba McCord.

I had broken the code of the warrior by getting beaten to often. I understood that.

Then it really hit the fan. Jimmy Gene's dad walked into the old cabin one day and caught us in bed together. And, true to the macho code, he went and told old Bubba.

I figured old Bubba would come after me, and, to tell the truth, I hoped he would. I had sweet dreams about kicking the daylights out of Bubba McCord. But he didn't do that. What he did was go to the plant and tell his friends about his wife and the football coach. Yeah, that was the dumbest thing he could have done, but I've learned not to try and predict anyone's reaction to trauma.

Especially not Jimmy Gene's.

Bubba got drunk one night, and commenced to beat Jimmy Gene. That's when she blew him away with the shotgun he cleaned every week.

Karankawa County mostly loved it all. Still love it. I mean, how could anything be sweeter at the Karankawa Drugstore? The foot-

136

ball coach, the board member who—justifiably—fired him, and the scarlet woman who killed her husband with his own shotgun.

It's not hard to imagine the stories Karankawa Countians tell about Jimmy Gene.

But none of them recognized the culprit in all of it like Jimmy Gene did. It was clear as could be to her, and she explained it to me when I visited her at the prison up at Huntsville.

"I could have competed with another woman, sweet boy," she told me. "I decided that when you first went up to the university. But that wasn't the problem. What I couldn't compete with, even when we were children, was the damned football. It was the football that took you away, and the football that brought you back to me. And it was the damned football that was taking you away again.

"It was the damned way—that *place*—we grew up in. The society that taught you and me and even Bubba, in a different way—see Bubba was *supposed* to wear a hardhat every day—how *it* thought we should live.

"When that prosecuter asked me if I had ever thought about killin' Bubba before, I just didn't know how to answer. Because Bubba sort of stood for that whole society. And God knows I wanted to kill it. Bubba was hurtin' me and he was handy. But I'm not sure whether I killed Bubba, or Karankawa County killed him, or the football killed him, or you killed him."

I left Karankawa County after that. Just drove away to another coaching job—it's all I know how to do.

Jimmy Gene hanged herself in her cell a few weeks later. And I'm writing all this just to set the story straight, so all Karankawa County can know the truth.

(*Oh Jimmy Gene, Jimmy Gene. Where are you now? Can you stop and pet dogs, and watch the leaves of touch-me-nots curl up like prayerful fingers? Is there someone to play catch with? God, I still love you, Jimmy Gene.*)

The Waxahachie Coke Bottle

I suppose some particular kinds of madness can kill you, after all. I can't prove it, of course, but regardless of what the Karankawa County coroner said, I figure it was being mad—slobbering, raving, glass-eyed mad—that killed Mr. Greenberry Turnbull. The coroner said exposure killed the old man; said there was no telling how long he had lain on the beach before I found him; said Mr. Turnbull was one huge, festered mosquito bite and the mosquitoes had made his eyes swell shut and his face bloat to twice its size.

But the coroner didn't get to talk to Mr. Turnbull right before he died like I did.

I ride my horse on the Texas beach every morning—a stretch near my ranch, southwest of Janus Point—so I can watch the sunrise. I never gave sunrises much thought before I began doing that. But after months of watching them I realized no two sunrises are exactly the same, and the concept staggered my imagination. For millions of years, day after day, every sunrise has been different; because of cloud formations and atmospheric conditions, I guess. I don't know how many *total* sunrises have appeared over that beach, but there must have been billions. And I'm sure they were all different.

It's a dirty beach, generally, because of washed-up garbage—big sheets of plastic, styrofoam blocks, plastic buckets, wine bottles, and wooden crates, among other things—are thrown overboard by off-shore drilling rigs and passing ships. And there's the regular junk dumped there by native Texans—abandoned cars, motorcycles, and old stoves and refrigerators. Then huge logs and whole trees with roots intact, washed in from the Yucatan, are strewn about. But they're in the natural order of things and would even be pleasing to the eye if it weren't for the human-made junk deposited all around them.

Mr. Turnbull was my Texas history teacher in high school back in the early fifties. We all laughed at him because he was so damned serious about Texas and what it was and what it should be and what it was going to be.

"They're poisoning Texas," he used to tell us. "They're gonna kill it dead-as-a-hammer."

"Mr. Turnbull is goofy as a peach-orchard boar," we usually said after his class was over.

"Texas should *itself* be nationalistic," Mr. Turnbull told us, "because it is America multiplied. It is wide and diverse, and those of us who sprung from its soil are *obligated*—yes, I said *obligated*—to guard its integrity and traditions zealously!"

"Goofy as a goose," we said.

None of us had the slightest notion what he was talking about, nor did we care.

I found Mr. Greenberry Turnbull lying on the beach in the fetal position beside a tree trunk from Yucatan. He scared the hell out of me, lying there white and bleached out like a big beached fish. He was moaning and talking to himself, and, at first, all I could understand was, ". . . Coke bottle."

Well, there were several bottles around him—pop bottles, wine bottles, small medicine bottles—and various rusty tin cans. But I wasn't too interested in them; all I wanted to do was get him on my horse and take him home.

Mr. Turnbull had always been a small man, never weighed more than one-thirty, I would guess, and he was dehydrated, so getting him on my big mare wasn't hard. He was able to help me a little, and I got on behind him, held him in the saddle, and we rode along, his head nodding with every step the horse took.

I could devote all my attention to Mr. Greenberry Turnbull because the gray mare, named Blue, knew the way as well as I did. She stepped around the refuse on the beach, planted her feet carefully beside the broken glass, and made wide circles around motorcycle skeletons. We made good time because she felt the urgency through my legs against her sides, I expect.

"Them skeeters sure played hell with your face, Mr. Turnbull," I told him. "How long you been on that beach? You sure look like hell."

He answered feebly, but I couldn't understand him at first. His voice was a squeaky whisper that scratched up from his throat, and I had to lean over and put my ear next to his face to hear. What he said made less sense than he had made as my teacher. But this is what I remember:

"My personality cracked, splintered into slivers, shattered like I was struck by the hammer of God, right on the top of the head. Then the black night air got painted with the red streak of a scream. And I didn't know where that scream originated. It didn't originate with anything human . . . or animal.

"It was like the devil screaming at the night sky. Or it might have been God screaming. Or it might have been two screams blended, harmonized, so they sounded like one. It might have been God and the devil screaming at each other in exactly the same instant, so you couldn't tell them apart and they sounded like one.

"It came from my throat, but that's not where it originated.

"I sat with the Gulf in front of me. I was aware, suddenly, very much aware, that there were two Texas rivers on my left, the Neches and Sabine. And on my right were the Trinity, Colorado, Brazos, Rio Grande . . . well, all of them. Then I was aware that those Texas rivers had been bringing—gushing into the Gulf for a million years— bringing bits and pieces of Texas with them.

"Bits and pieces from all over Texas were all around me . . .

"So I reached down on both sides of me and filled my hands with sand, and it trickled through my fingers in the dark. Back to where it came from.

"I chanted, 'Lubbock, San Antonio, Houston . . .' because the bottom of the Coke bottle said: Waxahachie, Texas."

Damn, I thought. He's crazier than ever. Gone around the bend, *plumb*. "You don't have to talk, Mr. Turnbull. Forget I asked you anything."

"But I didn't know if the Waxahachie Coke bottle had floated up on the beach from a Texas river, or if maybe some beach-goer had dropped it. And it bothered me to think it might have been brought by a snowbird from Michigan who just happened through Waxahachie on his way to the beach. It didn't seem right for that to be; because a Waxahachie Coke bottle should have been brought there by a Texan.

"Then everything got all screwed around and complicated, and I lay on my stomach and pulled the beach sand to me. I sat up and tried to hold it to my chest with both arms, holding it to me like a woman. But it kept trickling down my chest, onto my belly, then back down to the beach where it came from. I grabbed up more of it and tried to love it to me. And I sang, 'Fort Worth, Dallas, Laredo . . .'

"I could see every town in Texas all around me on the beach with their bright lights shining. I pulled them to me and tried to hold them, but they just kept trickling away and returning to the beach.

"Then God and the devil painted the night with that scream . . ."

That's all Mr. Greenberry Turnbull said before he passed out in my saddle and I took him home and called the ambulance.

He died in the hospital the next day, while I stood outside the emergency room and waited. Like a damned fool.

"He was goofy as a goose," I told the doctor after Mr. Turnbull died.

But the next morning, when I went to watch the sunrise on the beach, I looked for Coke bottles. And sure enough, I found Mr. Greenberry Turnbull's Waxahachie Coke bottle near where I had picked him up out of the sand. I still have it because . . . well, I figure any Texan who finds a Waxahachie Coke bottle should keep it.

Karankawa County was composed into type on a Compugraphic digital phototypesetter in eleven point Goudy Old Style with two points of spacing between the lines. Goudy Old Style was also selected for display. The book was typeset by Metricomp, Inc., printed offset by Thomson-Shore, Inc., and bound by John H. Dekker & Sons, Inc. The paper on which this book is printed carries acid-free characteristics for an effective life of at least three hundred years.

TEXAS A&M UNIVERSITY PRESS : COLLEGE STATION